Billionaire Undone

THE BILLIONAIRE'S OBSESSION

Travis

D1514059

CP/494

Billionaire Undone

Copyright © 2014 by J. S. Scott

Copy Editing by Roroblu's Mum
Proof Editing by Faith Williams – Atwater Group
Cover by Cali MacKay – Covers by Cali

ISBN: 978-1-939962-48-5 (Print)
ISBN: 978-1-939962-47-8 (E-Book)

Author Note

This book is for all my wonderful readers who wanted to know who Travis really is behind his cool mask and his sarcasm. This story is for you. There's always been so much more to him than you might think. I hope he surprises you all. Thank you for your support and enthusiasm. You'll never know how much it means to me.

Contents

Prologue

Shit! I'm late. I'm late.

Alison Caldwell nearly tripped on her high heels as she vaulted up the steps of her newly purchased home, desperate to get to her second job on time. The evening before, she and her fiancé, Rick, had spent the first night in their new home celebrating, and she'd forgotten to take her clothes for her second job with her when she'd left this morning.

Thank God she was almost done with her crazy schedule, her life finally totally on track because Rick had just graduated from dental school and was set to start his first job at an already thriving practice.

"I can do this for just a little while longer," she whispered to herself, putting her key into the door of the two-story home, a house she had financed herself because Rick's credit wasn't great, and even though she had been helping him through school for the last five years, he still had some significant student loans.

Her heels slipped again as she hit the foyer, the smooth stone tile making her shoes skid. *Damn heels!* If she didn't have to wear the stupid things to feel taller next to her billionaire boss from Hell, her feet wouldn't ache as badly as they did right now.

Ally yanked the offending footwear from her feet in the foyer, and climbed the carpeted stairs quickly, unbuttoning her conservative blouse and the back of her skirt as she went, to save time.

This was the way her life had been for the last few years, since she'd taken an extra job to help get Rick through school. But it would pay off. She knew it would. Her life plan was exactly the way it should be, her and Rick's small wedding being only a little more than a month away. They rarely saw each other because of her schedule, but she knew the sacrifice would pay off. They'd needed more income, and she had provided it, even though working two jobs was nearly killing her. Very shortly, she'd have her chance to go back to school and finish her MBA. That was the plan, the agreement they'd made when it was apparent that she and Rick couldn't both go to school at the same time. It had made sense, putting her degree off first. Rick would make more money than she could right out of school, and her job at Harrison Corporation paid well for a woman who hadn't actually finished her MBA. Unfortunately, keeping her position there came with a price; she actually had to work for Travis Harrison.

Releasing her hair from the confining clip as she went down the hallway to the master bedroom, Ally tried to put Travis out of her mind. They'd argued during the day, and he had fired her...yet again. Not that she took that threat seriously anymore. Travis Harrison fired her on a daily basis, and then proceeded to pile a bunch of work on her to complete the next day. But that part of her day was over, and she needed to get to Sully's Oasis, her evening job. And she was already late, and Travis was irritating as hell every single day. It wasn't like that was anything new, or something that was going to change anytime soon.

As Ally approached the bedroom door, she heard voices—one male voice she recognized very well, and a female voice that she didn't. She a heard a passionate groan from Rick, a sound she'd never heard before, and a responding husky female moan. The door wasn't completely closed, and she nudged her foot against the wood, swinging the door wide open.

There, in the middle of the brand new king-sized bed that she and Rick had slept on for the first time just the night before, was her fiancé. His head was thrown back in passionate abandon, a look of ecstasy on his face that she'd never seen before. The woman, naked and on her hands and knees in front of him, moaned again, the couple oblivious of her presence. Obviously, Rick hadn't planned on her coming back to the house before she went to her second job. She usually didn't, going straight from Harrison to Sully's.

Ally stared in morbid fascination, watching as the man she'd been involved with and had trusted for the last five years, killed her devotion with every thrust of his hips, every slap of his groin against the woman's bare ass. And as every bit of her love for him drained away, so came the realization that even after five years, *this* Rick was a complete stranger.

Who was this man, and what had happened to her solemn, quiet fiancé who made love to her infrequently because he was always too tired? She hadn't gotten much more than a peck on the cheek from him for the last two years. And even when they'd actually had a sex life, it wasn't one with this kind of furious frenzy that appeared to transform him into a man she had never known.

She'd always made excuses for the reasons why their relationship wasn't great. It was just that they were both working so hard, and things would change once they'd gotten through this difficult portion of their lives.

I never knew him.

Ally walked forward in a daze, tearing her eyes from the sight on the bed, crossing the room to pick up the jeans, t-shirt, and sneakers that she wore for her job at Sully's.

"Ally," Rick gasped heavily, finally noticing she was in the room.

Ally held up her hand. "Don't mind me. I just need my clothes to go to work to support you while you're screwing another woman. Do proceed. I've heard coitus interruptus is terribly uncomfortable." And she should know. How many times had Rick either stopped or left her unfulfilled back when they'd actually had sex? More times than she could count, but she'd always made excuses for his actions before. After seeing the sight she'd just observed, she knew what an idiot she'd been. It wasn't that he hadn't wanted sex; he just hadn't wanted it with *her*.

Ally didn't look in Rick's direction again. She didn't want to see him or the slender beauty he'd just been screwing. Her clothing in hand, Ally walked out the bedroom door, closing it behind her. Tearing off her conservative daytime attire as fast as she possibly could, she yanked on her bar attire, gathered her dirty clothes and dropped them in the second bathroom hamper on her way to the stairs, her sneakers in her hand.

"Ally, wait."

Ignoring Rick's voice as he shot out of the bedroom, she quickly pulled on the comfortable canvas shoes in the foyer.

"You can't just leave like this. I can explain," Rick yelled desperately from upstairs, hanging over the railing.

Like there was really *any* reasonable explanation for what she'd just witnessed? Raising her voice just loud enough to be heard, she answered, "Get out. I want you gone by the time I get home from work. If you aren't, I'll call the police."

"We've been together for five years. That has to count for something," Rick appealed.

It did count for a lot, and none of it pleasant. Ally had worked her ass off every day, and had missed her chance to finish college because of those five torturous years spent working to make sure Rick had a career. She'd made a plan, stuck to every single thing she vowed to do so she and Rick could have the perfect life together. She'd always told herself if she could just hold things together while he was in school, she would have her chance. And now, that carefully planned outline had been erased like it had never happened, leaving her nowhere. Just years of empty space.

Ally didn't respond, nor did she look up at the man to whom she'd given five long years of her life. He didn't deserve it.

I have to keep moving. I'll survive.

Exiting the house, she closed the door behind her. She was in her car and on her way to Sully's before she could see Rick come bursting out the front door in only a hastily donned pair of jeans, cursing because she was already gone.

Ally arrived at Sully's ten minutes late for work, but she did her job, no one even suspecting that her entire world had just tumbled down around her, her plans for her future gone.

When she arrived back home, exhausted, Rick was gone. She dragged her tired body to one of the extra bedrooms, her body and mind completely drained. Ally knew if she stopped for even a moment to think about what had happened, she'd lose it entirely, and that wasn't something she could afford to do right now.

Blanking her mind, pushing all thoughts of the past aside, she let her worn-out body succumb to a mind-numbing sleep.

Chapter 1

One Month Later

Ally Caldwell never needed to actually *see* her boss, Travis Harrison, to know he was making his way to his office. He was like a force of nature that everyone shied away from, the whole upper floor of the luxurious high-rise Harrison building going from a buzz of activity to absolute silence whenever *Travis the Tyrant* entered the top floor from the elevator, every employee freezing like a deer in the headlights until he passed, each one breathing a sigh of relief as he moved by them without acknowledging their presence. Nobody wanted to be singled out by Travis Harrison, because it usually meant trouble.

Ally sighed, beleaguered. Most days, she thrived on doing verbal battle with one of the most obnoxious men on the planet. But today just wasn't one of those days. Since her world had collapsed last month, she didn't have the energy or the desire to do battle with Travis anymore, but she did it anyway, just because he could be such an asshole.

Pushing her glasses back onto her face and turning back to her computer, she murmured to herself:

"Five...

"Four...

"Three...

"Two...

"One..."

"Coffee, Alison," Travis's booming voice demanded right on time as he strode through the automatic doors to his spacious private office, walking purposefully into the reception area without even looking at her.

Ally rolled her eyes. In the four years that she'd worked for Travis, she hadn't fetched him coffee for the last three years, but he never stopped trying. "I'd love some, Mr. Harrison," she replied, not looking up from her computer screen. "Cream only, please," she reminded him politely, like she did every single working day. Some days he cursed her; other days he would grudgingly get his own coffee but wouldn't say a word. Ally wondered which way it would go today.

Travis hesitated at the door to his private office, turning around to glare at her. "Four damn years, and I still can't get a cup of coffee in my own office?" he complained obstinately.

Ally swiveled in her chair and folded her hands on her desk. "Of course you can," she answered reasonably. "I made a pot this morning." She gestured to the small kitchen behind her. "And I only stopped fetching for you like an obedient dog three years ago."

Maybe if you'd thanked me just once, I'd still be doing it. Jackass!

Travis straightened his already pristine tie as he moved across the room, entering the kitchen without another word. Ally cringed as she heard the slamming of glass on glass as Travis poured coffee. Really, maybe she shouldn't have stopped getting his coffee for him years ago; his awkward skills in the kitchen had cost Harrison a lot of money in glassware replacements. But she'd made a stand, refusing to do his bidding like a personal servant because that was exactly how he'd treated her. She worked her butt off to do good work for Travis

Harrison as a secretary and assistant, hoping that maybe she could use her work experience at Harrison to go back for her MBA, but she drew the line at doing *everything* he demanded now. Ally had learned a long time ago that if she gave in to Travis just a little, he'd push her to the limit, continue to treat her like a personal servant. And she had way too many other responsibilities now at Harrison, and more important duties than fetching his damn coffee. So she'd stopped fetching for him altogether unless it was related to business and not a personal need, rather than drive herself crazy trying to please him. There *was* no pleasing Travis Harrison, and the words "please" and "thank you" simply didn't exist in his vocabulary, even when dealing with his peers. Just the fact that she still had her job was testament to her value here at Harrison Corporation, which she supposed was the only validation she was ever going to receive. She may not have applied to an MBA program, but she'd learned enough in her undergrad work to know exactly how to make herself nearly indispensable to Travis, and she'd done it in a year. And the moment she realized just how valuable she was as an employee, she'd stopped taking a lot of his crap.

Travis exited the kitchen, slamming a mug on her desk as he passed. "You can add your own damn cream," he said abruptly, moving toward his personal office with his own coffee as he added, "I'll need—"

"Your schedule for the day is on your computer, along with the information you requested yesterday," she finished for him.

"And I have a meeting—"

"With Jason Sutherland? I know. It's already on your schedule. He called me." *He's a considerate billionaire.* Ally smiled as she picked up her mug of coffee and the two packets of creamer Travis had left on her desk. He'd even added a stir stick. Obviously he was playing nice today...for now. Lately, he'd been doing that more and more often. Not to say that he was exactly *pleasant*. Today, he was obviously in a mellow mood, which meant he was merely hard to get along with. No doubt, he'd eventually show his "bastard" side. He always did.

"Sutherland called you?" Travis asked irritably.

"This morning before you got in." Ally looked directly at Travis, something that was harder to do when both of them were standing. He was so tall, she was usually staring at his massive chest and shoulders, and she wore the highest heels she could tolerate to bring her up a little taller. Any advantage she could get when dealing with him was another weapon in her arsenal.

His appearance was impeccable and flawless as usual. Travis's twin, Kade, liked to tease Travis about his dark, boring suits, but nobody could fill out a designer suit quite the way Travis Harrison did. Sure, the immaculate clothing he wore was always dark, just like him. But the dark gray suit he was wearing today fit to perfection, accentuating broad shoulders and covering what Ally already knew—from seeing him in more casual attire or without his suit jacket—was a majorly ripped physique. He didn't have one single raven-colored hair out of place, and his dark, chocolate eyes were way too sharp for her comfort.

"Mr. Sutherland thought it would be nice if I knew about the meeting you two set up since I do your daily schedule. I thought it was very thoughtful of him to contact me," Ally replied sweetly, her real purpose of the comment to point out how considerate Travis *wasn't*.

Ally knew *about* Jason Sutherland, but had never met the investment icon billionaire in person. He'd been very kind on the phone, and had told her he'd contacted Travis directly because he was interested in donating and handling the investments for the new charity Travis was starting for women who were victims of domestic abuse. Travis's friend, Simon Hudson, had spoken of the charity to his college buddy, Grady, a well-known philanthropist from the wealthy East Coast Sinclair family. Grady had come on board, and had mentioned the charity to his childhood friend—Jason—who for some reason, had taken an interest in the project and wanted to be part of the new foundation.

"Show him in as soon as he gets here." Travis turned and entered his office, closing the door behind him.

"Yes, sir," she muttered irritably at the closed door of Travis's office, throwing the best military salute she could in his general direction mockingly, knowing very well that the gesture irritated the hell out of her boss. It felt good to do something that annoyed him, even if he wasn't there to see it.

Ally shook the two packets of creamer, opened them, and dumped them into her coffee with a thoughtful look, lost in her own thoughts as she twirled the stir stick in the hot liquid.

It wasn't that she didn't like Travis. Well…not exactly. *Like* was too tepid of a word for Travis Harrison; he inspired strong emotions in his employees, everything from terror to admiration. Never really a likable man, Travis maintained a deliberate distance from everyone, so Ally did everything she could to shake him out of his self-contained shell, which vexed the hell out of him. Sometimes, she preferred his anger to his icy indifference. Travis was too serious, too somber, and completely humorless. Maybe she shouldn't perturb him so often, but it was difficult not to want to take a peek at the man who lived beneath his hardened exterior. So far, all she'd gotten was his outrage for the last three years. She'd spent the first year as his employee just grateful for a job, wanting to please him so she could keep the fantastic salary he was paying her, and possibly use the job experience some day to apply for an MBA program. Within a year, she knew he'd never fire her because he needed her too much, although he'd never admit it. After that, she'd made it her mission to get a rise out of Travis Harrison, anything that would take the haunted look from his eyes that she noticed occasionally, though he wasn't even aware that it was there.

He'd hate that, knowing that if one looked hard enough, they could see he had vulnerabilities.

"Four years, and I still haven't completely figured the man out," she muttered to herself, blowing on her coffee before taking a sip of the hot beverage. He was grim and poker-faced, unless he was pissed off. Personally, she preferred his ire to the unhappy restlessness she sensed in him. Maybe most people thought Travis Harrison had it all, but Ally didn't think so, and she never gave up trying to see who the man was beneath the asshole exterior.

Certainly, he did have admirable qualities. He paid as much attention to his charities as he did to his actual business, choosy about which organizations he dumped a fortune into. But Travis Harrison did nothing halfheartedly. Once he'd decided on his worthy causes, he worked as hard on making those charitable organizations successful as he did his business deals. Ally admired that about Travis. Unfortunately, all too often, he was also a complete jerk. Could any man really be as completely dark as her boss, yet give so much to help other people? She'd been asking that same question over and over for years, but hadn't yet discovered the answer.

"Ms. Caldwell!" Travis bellowed from his office, not bothering to use the intercom. Not that he needed it.

Ally stood, resigned. She'd been waiting for his familiar summoning roar, already knowing what he wanted. Yanking her too-tight, navy pencil skirt down over her curvy hips so the hem would fall back to her knees, she cursed herself for her poor diet and lack of exercise. Her crazy schedule was definitely starting to show in her appearance, and she'd never exactly been a looker in the first place. The skirt had fit just fine a few years ago, and she hadn't exactly been thin then either. Now, every single item she owned was too tight, and she definitely didn't have the money to buy new clothes.

"Diet," she uttered emphatically, tucking a few stray locks of hair behind her ears that had escaped from the thick, blonde French braid that hung down her back. She placed her reading glasses carefully on her desk, knowing she wouldn't need them for this confrontation with Travis.

Swinging the door open, she entered, leaning against the door to close it. "You needed something, Mr. Harrison?" she asked with saccharine sweetness.

"What the hell is this?" He was waving around a sheet of paper, giving her an angry stare.

"It's a reminder about my vacation. I put in the request nearly a year ago," she told him calmly, approaching his desk.

"The answer is no," Travis replied in an irritatingly voice of a dictator, tearing up the reminder and dropping it into the trash.

"It wasn't a request. I *requested* a year ago. I was just reminding you that you're going to have a temp to replace me for two weeks."

"Not possible," he dismissed. "I'll be in Colorado one of those weekends, and I need you there."

Ally gritted her teeth. "I put in for that time for my wedding. You've known that for a damn year." She leaned over his desk, placing her palms on the edge, furious now. "I haven't taken a single day off in the four years I've worked here. I cash in my vacation time and take the money. Just once, I actually *need* the time off. I'm taking it."

Travis folded his arms stubbornly. "Making coffee might not be in your job description, Ms. Caldwell, but traveling with me when I need you definitely *is* a condition of your employment. And I haven't needed that assistance in the four years you've been working for me."

Travis was right. He had never asked her to travel with him, and it *was* part of her job should the need arise. He did everything alone. So why did he need her now? "This is important," she muttered.

Ally knew she needed the time off for her sanity. She needed to rip the scab off her wounds and deal with the mess Rick had left behind. Her credit card statements had come yesterday, and she was reminded that she'd never bothered to cancel Rick's user privileges. The bastard had charged up the cards immediately after she'd closed the sale on the house and caught the asshole cheating on her, probably to buy expensive gifts for his new girlfriend. In her wildest imagination, she never would have thought that Rick would do that to her. Of course, she hadn't thought she'd find him banging another woman in their home either. And the house needed to go up for sale. Not only did she *not* need the reminder of her failed engagement and five wasted years, but there was no way she could carry the expensive mortgage without him contributing for any length of time. Not with the other debt he'd run up in her name. And she didn't want to be house poor, killing herself working two jobs just for a home she no longer wanted. This wasn't where her life was supposed to be. She was supposed to have a fiancé—soon-to-be husband—who was finally working in his profession, contributing to their life together.

Instead, she had a mess to sort out, her dream of finally having a normal life completely shattered.

Don't think about it right now. You'll figure it all out when you get a minute to breathe. Focus on work.

Travis snorted unpleasantly. "You're marrying a loser. Better if you don't get married. You'll be divorced within a year."

Ally gritted her teeth, fuming. How many times had Travis said that? And God, it really annoyed the crap out of her that he was actually right. "I'm not getting married," she answered, her voice clipped.

Travis's head jerked away from his computer, giving her an intense stare. "Since when?"

"Since about a month ago, when I found my supposed future husband boinking some young, attractive, probably barely legal, big-breasted Barbie doll in our brand new bed," she answered loudly, her words completely uncensored. Travis made her crazy, but for the first time in four years, she found herself genuinely losing control. "So excuse me if I need some goddamn vacation time that I've genuinely earned from your company to deal with *that*. I don't have a second to breathe between working here and at Sully's. I have personal things I have to take care of. I have a house I now need to sell, and I need to bail myself out of credit card and other debt that I had no part in creating." Ally gulped and took a deep breath, panic beginning to swamp her for the very first time. "I need some time to figure everything out." Where did she go from here? Her whole life had revolved around her plan and Rick's education for years.

"You didn't tell me," Travis answered calmly.

Ally threw her hands up in the air, trying to keep herself from going for Travis's throat. Like he really invited warm and fuzzy conversation? He spent most of his time barking orders at her. "I didn't realize that I needed to share my personal life with my self-centered bastard of a boss. I keep my troubles to myself because I know that's the way you like it. You pay me to work, and I do my job. Now I want to take my earned vacation time." Had she really just called Travis a bastard? They fought constantly, and she'd certainly wanted to say those words to his face about a million times in the past, but she'd never been *that* blunt or unprofessional. She really was beginning to lose it. "Please. Just give me the time off. I'll come back a better person for it."

"He hurt you," Travis stated neutrally.

Ally dropped into the chair in front of Travis's desk, depleted. "My whole life revolved around his career for years. I stopped going to college after my bachelor's degree instead of trying to go on for my MBA so he could finish first. It made sense at the time. Or I thought it did. I sacrificed everything I wanted, but I had a plan to make everything work out. I'd work hard, help him finish school, and then it would be my turn. Except, now that it's supposed to be my turn, it isn't," she answered quietly, her anger spent.

"I didn't realize you worked another job. What do you do?" Travis leaned back in his chair, but he didn't look away from her, his dark eyes watching her intently.

"I'm a bartender. I work at Sully's Oasis almost every night of the week. I started as a cocktail waitress, and the owner taught me to make drinks. Eventually, I got good at it. The bartending pays better."

Travis lifted an eyebrow. "Better than I pay you?"

"No. Better than being a cocktail waitress. I had to work my way up to bartending." It taken her two years, but she'd gotten a raise at Sully's. "The tips are good. You pay me a very good salary. I could never match it with bartending. But the extra job helps to pay the bills. I need to sell the house, get clear of the debt my cheating fiancé racked up, and get rid of the extra job so I can go back to school part-time."

"You look tired, Alison," Travis observed, his eyes traveling over her face.

"I've been exhausted for years. I'm used to it." Ally laughed, trying to make light of the situation. This wasn't the type of conversation she usually had with Travis, and she was feeling raw and awkward. She was much more comfortable fighting with him.

"She better be a good temp." Travis finally spoke after a moment of silence. "I still need you in Colorado, but you can have the time off before we leave. Just bump it up a week so you're back before I have to go. I assume since you're not getting married, what time you take off doesn't really matter."

Ally looked at Travis in surprise. "*He* is a very good temp, and that would mean I'd have to go on vacation next week."

"Then go." Travis shrugged.

"What are we doing in Colorado?" she asked curiously.

Travis grimaced. "A fundraiser. I need an escort."

Ally gaped at him. "I'm not going as your date to a fundraiser. That's personal. I thought you had business there."

"I do. And you aren't technically my date. I have to attend this function, and I don't want to go alone," Travis rumbled. "It's not that difficult. You go. You talk nicely to people and try not to call them self-centered bastards. And then you eat and drink whatever they have to offer. Tate Colter has been a business associate and a friend of mine for years. He agreed to do this charity ball only if I'd come to Colorado because I haven't visited for a while. He wants me to be there. Going alone would be—" Travis coughed before finishing. "Awkward."

"Why?" Ally crossed her arms in front of her. There was nothing strange about going to a fundraiser alone. There had to be something Travis wasn't telling her. "You attend these types of things all the time. You don't need me there."

"This one is...different," Travis said hesitantly. "I just need you to be there, Alison. It *is* technically business. Your presence is required. The temp can stay and hold down the fort with Kade while we're gone."

Ally eyed Travis curiously, wondering what he *wasn't* saying. "I don't have the necessary attire for that kind of function. I've never needed anything but office attire."

"I'll provide it. You're dismissed back to your duties." He waved a hand at her like she was a pesky fly.

God, Ally hated it when Travis did that. She felt like a naughty schoolgirl. "And how long will we be gone?"

"Leave Friday, return Monday. The actual ball is on Saturday night," Travis answered absently, as though he had already put the whole thing out of his mind.

Ally stood, brushing imaginary wrinkles away on her tight skirt and tugging it down her hips. "Diet," she reminded herself, turning to leave the office. She wanted to argue with Travis, but she couldn't. He'd never asked her to travel with him, and it was part of her job as his assistant. The fact that Travis was a loner, and preferred it that way, was one of the reasons she was actually able to work a second job. He was usually alone, and didn't feel the need for an entourage. And he never required anything from her outside of work hours. She'd do this for him just because he wasn't demanding in that way, and he very well could have been. Somehow, although he was making light of it, it seemed important to him, and he'd never asked her to travel to events with him before.

"Totally unnecessary, Alison," Travis said in a low, graveled voice so quietly that Ally almost didn't hear him.

She turned back to him. "What's unnecessary?"

"You don't need to diet." Travis scowled at her.

Ally rolled her eyes. "Yeah. Sure. My gorgeous body certainly didn't keep my fiancé from banging another woman in our bed," she answered facetiously, surprising herself again by the words that popped out of her mouth. She might do battle with Travis fairly often, but it had never gotten this personal.

Travis rose slowly, his liquid, fierce gaze never leaving her as he crossed the room unhurriedly, stopping right in front of her. Ally stepped back, trapping herself between Travis's massive body and the door as he stepped forward again. His masculine scent filled the air around her and she almost sighed when she inhaled the intoxicating smell. She didn't get this close to him very often, but whenever she did, her knees got weak just from the virile, musky male scent that emanated from his body like pheromones, beckoning her to get close enough to wallow in him. Travis might be a stubborn ass most of the time, but one thing Ally couldn't deny was that he was a gorgeous, potent, testosterone-overloaded male ass.

Travis placed a palm on each side of her head, leaning down until Ally shivered as his warm breath caressed her ear.

"Your *ex*-fiancé was and is an idiotic fool. You, Alison, have the kind of soft, feminine body any man wants beneath him when he sinks his cock into a woman's body. Every single thing about you is perfect." His voice was husky, warm, and mesmerizing. "If he'd been smarter, he would have made you come, given you exactly what you wanted until you were so addicted to him that you'd never walk away, and he'd never want another woman when he had you in his bed."

Ally nearly moaned against Travis's shoulder, the seductive voice in her ear enthralling her. "He didn't do that," she admitted, leaning her head back against the door. Rick hadn't given a shit whether she was satisfied or not.

Travis straightened, looking down at her from his towering height, his face changing to a mask of indifference. "Then he didn't deserve you. Actually, he never did." He stepped back, allowing space to open the door.

Ally fumbled with the door, flustered. What the hell had just happened to her? She scurried out, not looking behind her as she closed the door to Travis's office, her hands shaking, her nipples hard and sensitive just from the sheer eroticism of Travis's low, seductive voice whispering naughty words into her ear.

She sat down at her desk, dazed and confused, wondering if her overactive imagination had just conjured up that particular moment in time. Travis Harrison had never looked at her with anything other than irritation. And he'd certainly never said anything that made her hot and bothered in less than a few seconds.

Sipping her lukewarm coffee, she put her reading glasses back on and turned to her computer, giving herself a mental slap to stop thinking about Travis. After all, he hadn't even touched her. It was nothing to make a big deal over. So, he'd thrown her a very strange compliment, but at the end of the day, it didn't really change any-thing. Travis was just...different today, and in a very odd mood. Shaking her head, she got back to work.

Chapter 2

Jason Sutherland was in an excellent mood as he strolled into Travis Harrison's top floor office, and he smiled when he saw a pretty blonde woman sitting behind a desk right inside the door. She had to be Ally, Travis's assistant with whom he'd spoken earlier that morning. Her looks were just as appealing as her voice. Not that he'd ever notice her in a romantic way. But she appeared to be just as charming as she'd sounded on the phone.

"Mr. Sutherland?" The woman rose from the chair and gave him a friendly smile that surprised him.

He was used to a sly, artificially bright welcome from women, and looks that sized up him and his bank account at the same time. Hope Sinclair, Grady's younger sister, was the only woman who had ever really treated him like a person rather than an eligible billionaire. In fact, Hope had always treated him with a little too much nonchalance, and way too much like an older brother for his taste—until *the incident* that had happened at Christmas when he'd seen her in Amesport. "Ally." He grinned back at her, taking the hand she offered him in welcome. "It's very nice to meet you in person. Please call me Jason."

Ally took her hand from his and nodded as she answered. "It's nice to meet you, too. Thank you for calling this morning. Mr. Harrison is expecting you. I'll call him."

"He's already here," a low, irritated baritone announced from the other side of the office. "Come in, Sutherland."

Jason looked toward the voice, feeling underdressed in a pair of jeans and a buttoned-down shirt when he looked at Travis Harrison. Grady had already warned him that Travis was an intimidating son of a bitch, according to Simon, and now Jason knew why. The dark look on Travis's face was almost homicidal, and Jason had to work to keep a straight face as Travis glanced at Ally in a proprietary manner and then back at him again. Really, Jason didn't care that Travis was openly an asshole, and wasn't the least bit daunted. He'd rather have a man be openly hostile than have him smile to his face and then stab him in the back. He had a feeling he'd always know exactly where he stood with Travis Harrison, and that was fine by him.

He winked at Ally as he passed her desk and sauntered into Travis's office.

"She's off-limits," Travis growled at him after he'd closed the office door.

"She married?" Jason asked innocently, taking a seat in front of Travis's desk.

"No," Travis rumbled, sitting down behind the massive oak desk.

"Involved?" he pushed, smirking as Travis scowled at him.

"No."

"A relative?" Jason knew damn well she wasn't related to Travis, but he was starting to really have fun yanking Harrison's chain. He guessed that misery really did love company.

"Hell, no," Travis replied, disgusted. "But if you touch her, I'll kill you."

Bingo. Jason knew he'd hit a nerve. "She's very nice, and very pretty—"

"I told you—"

"But I'm not interested," Jason finished with a grin.

"You gay?" Travis asked, actually looking hopeful.

Jason shook his head, nearly hating to squash Travis's relief that he wasn't heterosexual. Shit, Travis had a real thing for Ally. Obviously, the man thought that any guy who looked at her wanted to fuck her because he was so obsessed with the idea himself. And Jason knew exactly how that felt. "No. But my affections are otherwise engaged."

Travis picked up a pen and twirled it thoughtfully between his fingers, scrutinizing Jason so thoroughly that it almost made him want to squirm. Hell, Jason had gone rounds with the biggest boys out there, sometimes more than once, but Travis was in a whole different league. Not meaner, exactly. Just…different.

"I didn't know you were engaged, or even had a girlfriend," Travis admitted, dropping the pen on his desk.

"I'm not. It's…complicated," Jason confessed, leaning back in the chair and giving Travis a disgruntled look.

"Ah…unrequited lust. You want to fuck her, but she doesn't want you. It sucks, doesn't it?" Travis finally commiserated, shooting Jason a knowing look.

That wasn't exactly how it had gone with Hope, but close enough for him to answer, "Big time," Jason affirmed, starting to feel a strange affinity with Travis. The poor guy had a serious case of blue balls over his secretary, and that situation was obviously uncomfortable because Travis had to be in close proximity to Ally all of the time.

"So how serious are you about managing this foundation with us?" Travis asked, changing the subject, obviously satisfied that Jason wasn't going to pursue Ally.

"My time is valuable, and I flew here from the East Coast. I'm extremely serious. I'm not only willing to donate, but work the investments to keep the charity solvent as long as the overall plans are workable." Jason wanted to be involved, needed to do something valuable. He had more money than he could ever possibly spend over several lifetimes, even if he bought every toy he wanted. He admitted to himself that he was restless; he needed something more important to work on than just increasing his own wealth.

"It's workable. I figured out most of the plans myself," Travis answered arrogantly, pushing a thick folder across the desk. "We can go over to Kade's office and go over it with him. This is an important project for both he and his wife, Asha."

Jason stood, ready to get busy. He needed the distraction right now. "Kade Harrison. He was a hell of a quarterback," Jason said, following Travis to the door of his office.

"Still is," Travis replied, opening the door to his office, and turning back to Jason. "He just doesn't play anymore. Hell of a businessman, too."

Jason smiled at Travis's back as they left the office. Travis Harrison might be raw, but he obviously was fiercely protective and proud of those he cared about. As far as Jason was concerned, that type of loyalty was better than false charm, and rare in the circles that they both traveled in.

Ally smiled at Jason as he walked past her desk, and he grinned back at her, wondering absently if she knew that she had such a ferocious protector, and that Travis's feelings for her, like his own for Hope, were about as far from brotherly as feelings could get.

"I'll be in Kade's office," Travis snapped at Ally.

Judging by Travis's not-so-gentle treatment of his assistant, Jason doubted she knew a damn thing. But he nearly laughed when he saw her dismissive attitude, acknowledging Travis's comment with a small nod, but not appearing the least bit afraid of him. In fact, she'd almost ignored him, not even looking up from whatever work she was doing on the computer.

She challenges him.

Jason smirked as he followed the other man down the hall to Kade's office, wondering just how long it would take Travis to crack.

She isn't getting married. She broke up with her asshole of a fiancé. She's available. She's available. She's available.

The mantra drummed in Travis's brain as he drove his Hennessey Venom GT around his racetrack for the first time, testing out the speed and handling of the new vehicle that had just arrived earlier in the day. Ordinarily, he would have been itching to get the vehicle up to the fastest speed possible, completely focused on examining its capabilities, but today wasn't an ordinary day.

Today is the day I found out that Alison Caldwell isn't engaged anymore.

Driving at deadly speeds and thinking about Ally Caldwell really didn't mix, but his cock was hard, and it wasn't from the throbbing engine of the vehicle he was currently driving. It was her fault; his erection was due to the fact that the blonde menace in a tight skirt was actually single for the first time since she'd become his employee.

His fingers tightened around the steering wheel as he expertly maneuvered around a curve, barely lowering his speed as he hit the straightaway again. God, the vehicle was sweet, but all he could think about was how much sweeter fucking Ally would be, having her panting his name beneath him as he made her come over and over, until all she could think about was him.

Four years and thirty-two days he'd dreamed about just that scenario; one thousand, four hundred and ninety torturous days of blue balls that no other woman could cure. Except her. He'd been in trouble since the day she'd walked into his office for an interview, slightly breathless and nervous. His dick had twitched in his pants immediately, making him want to reach out, pull her onto his lap, and make her even more breathless until they were both completely sated. Why in the hell he'd gone ahead and hired her he never understood. He must have been feeling masochistic, because her sweet, guileless beauty had haunted him every damn moment since the day he'd hired her. And her intelligence and sharp tongue both annoyed the shit out of him and challenged him. There was nothing more that he wanted than to tame the little tigress, make her yield to him until she purred.

I need to just fuck her and get her out of my system.

Rounding the curve again, Travis accelerated, moving the car to an elevated speed after getting used to the feel of the handling. He tried to concentrate on his new vehicle. Having paid well over a million dollars for the speed demon, he should be more enthusiastic about driving it. He had more expensive cars, but he'd wanted to add this particular vehicle to his collection for a while, had anticipated its arrival because it was so damn fast. Today, he wasn't getting the same high he usually did in acquiring one of the fastest vehicles in the world.

Because of her!

"Dammit!" he exploded, frustrated. He knew better than to drive like this when he wasn't concentrating. He slowed the vehicle down and finally pulled it into the garage, one of his mechanics waiting for him at the door.

"She's fast, boss, huh?" the mechanic asked excitedly.

"Very," Travis replied, leaving the engine running as he exited the vehicle. "Can you put her away for me, Henry? Take it for a spin if you want before you shut it down." He had certain people he trusted to drive his cars, and Henry was one of those few mechanics he'd trust with any of his vehicles.

"Thanks, boss," the older man said enthusiastically. "You leaving?"

"Yeah. I'll probably be back tomorrow night," Travis affirmed, heading toward his Ferrari F12, the car he had driven to the track. The Ferrari was fast, and it was comfortable. Since he generally didn't do suicidal speeds outside of the racetrack, he could appreciate the beauty of the Ferrari, but didn't require the acceleration some of his other cars gave him on the track.

"Kade will love this car," Henry commented as Travis walked away.

"He will. But I'm not letting him drive it," Travis replied wickedly, flashing Henry an evil grin. He knew Kade would be salivating over the Hennessey, but Kade had his own damn toys. The garage was full of expensive race cars and motorcycles. Maybe in a few months, Travis would break down and let Kade give it a try, but not on the track, and not at reckless speeds. Kade was an expert at handling bikes, but he wasn't as good with cars. The last thing Travis wanted was to see was Kade injured again. It had nearly killed him when his brother had had the accident that ended his pro football career. He couldn't watch his twin suffer like that again. It had taken Kade two years of rehab to even be functional and be able to walk without relying on crutches. Kade deserved every bit of happiness he was now experiencing with his wife, Asha, who was pregnant and expecting their first child.

Although Travis couldn't even begin to understand having that type of relationship with a woman, the same loving relationship his sister Mia had with her husband Max, he was good with it because his siblings were happy.

"He'll be mad," Henry warned.

Travis waved as he got into his F12. "He'll have to get over it," he replied gruffly, closing the door of the Ferrari and strapping himself in. He watched as Henry got into the Hennessey and entered the track, taking it easy with the expensive vehicle as he rounded the first lap.

I'm not going to do it. I'm not going to do it.

Travis wanted nothing more than to hightail it over to Sully's Oasis and see if Ally was okay. Yeah, she'd been okay for a few years now, but that had been before he knew that she worked there as a bartender, without a decent man in her life to watch out for her. Now, all he could think about was other men salivating over her as the drinks she served got them more and more drunk. Intoxicated guys were dangerous. Ally was dangerous to intoxicated men. *Fuck!* He wished his damn cock would just explode into tiny little pieces and put him out of his misery. He put his hand over the denim-clad bulge, wondering if it just might.

Night after night, all he could think about for the last four years was Ally going home to some other asshole, letting him touch her, fuck her until she screamed. Apparently, *that* hadn't happened. The bastard hadn't even appreciated what he had with Ally, while Travis would have given his right nut to have her in his bed. She'd never talked much about her fiancé, and now he knew why. Too damn tired from working two jobs, she probably did nothing but focus on work. God knew that she was a hard worker. He'd put her through the wringer over the years, and she'd never complained about her workload, never stopped the string of sassy remarks coming out of that sexy mouth of hers. Now, he regretted being so hard on her, but it had been his way of creating some kind of distance between the two of them.

He leaned his head back and closed his eyes, reliving the incident this morning, the mouthwatering fragrance he'd inhaled into his lungs when he'd gotten close to her. All he'd wanted was to freeze that moment, absorb the light, flowery, intoxicating scent of her skin until it filled every cell in his body. He wanted her just that damn desperately. Maybe Ally was a tough woman, but he'd seen the flash of vulnerability in her eyes hidden beneath her sarcastic comments this morning. And he hadn't liked it. How could she *not* know that she was probably every man's wet dream? He knew for a fact she was his *only* wet dream, had known it for the last four years and thirty-two days. That's how long he'd been beating off while fantasizing about Ally. He hadn't been able to stop himself from getting close to her after she'd let down her guard, letting her know how damn beautiful she was earlier today. Ally was a fighter, and he hated seeing that hurt look in her beautiful green eyes, unhidden by those sexy, naughty librarian glasses she wore every day that drove him half crazy. The glasses fueled his fantasy of stripping Ally of every prim and proper notion from her brain and making her come until she became a wanton woman, needing nothing except him. Was it the glasses she usually donned for most of the day that had kept him from noticing the dark circles under her eyes, and how tired she looked? Or maybe it was just the fact that his dick was hard every moment that she was in the same room with him, and he'd been too damn defensive to notice. Grudgingly, he admitted that fighting with her kept her at a distance, which he desperately needed. But even *that* wasn't really working anymore.

He'd barely contained himself from pummeling Jason Sutherland today, just because the guy smiled at Ally. Sutherland was supposedly an irresistible lure to women because of his golden good looks and money, and Travis didn't want the man—any man under the age of eighty—near Ally ever again. She'd just gotten rid of a loser. Not that Sutherland was a loser, and Travis had actually ended up liking the guy. But he didn't like Jason when he was touching Ally, and he hadn't liked her touching Sutherland either. The smile she had given Jason this morning had slammed him right in the gut, making him wonder why he'd never seen that relaxed, happy look directed at *him*.

Maybe because I'm an asshole whenever she's around? Admittedly, he was an asshole most of the time. Okay...maybe *all* of the time. But there was never a moment that he didn't feel out of control about Ally. He'd just learned to rein it in because she was involved with another guy. He hadn't had a choice. But had he known that she wasn't happy, what that bastard was putting her through, he might not have been as hesitant to poach on another man's territory. In fact, he would have done it quite happily and without remorse had he known that Ally wasn't being treated the way she deserved to be treated. She might piss him off more often than not, but he hated the thought of her not being treated right by a man who supposedly loved her.

He started the ignition, waiting for it to fire up. Maybe it would have been better if he hadn't known about her situation, if he was completely ignorant of the fact that her prick of an ex had hurt her. But now he did know, and it was driving him completely insane. She was working too hard, pushing herself too much. She could end up sick, collapse from exhaustion. Or some prick at the bar could decide she looked ripe for the picking. He was angry with himself that he hadn't noticed before because he was too busy trying to get a grip whenever she was near him.

I'm not going to do it. I'm not going to do it.

Everything she was going through at the moment could be easily solved, her bills could be paid, and he could pay for her house. Travis scowled. Well...maybe not *that* house. He didn't want her living in a home where her ex had banged another woman. *Stupid bastard!* But he could get her a different home. Hell, he could even help her get into an MBA program if that's what she wanted. He could do it with a simple phone call. For some unknown reason, all he really wanted to do was make her smile, have her look at him like she'd looked at Jason this morning.

I'm not going to do it. I'm not going to do it.

Shortly, he'd have to spend four days in her nearly constant company on the trip to Colorado. If she ever learned exactly why he needed her to be there, he'd get nothing but scorn and disbelief from her. He'd never tell her. That had been decided before he'd ever insisted on her being there. She'd never have to know.

He wondered irritably what in the hell had possessed him to give her two weeks off. He hadn't gone more than a few days without seeing her in the last four years. The office would probably fall apart while she was gone. Oh hell, who was he kidding? *He'd* probably fall apart. Being able to see her, even if they were throwing insults at each other, had been the only thing that had kept him balanced. And she'd still be working at the bar every night, with horny, inebriated men slobbering all over her.

I'm not going to do it. I'm not going to do it.

Nope. He *wasn't* going to do it. Travis Harrison did *not* do anything to draw attention to himself. Making a vow to himself and his brother after his parents had died, he'd clawed to get the Harrison name out of the gutter, make it respected again. And for the most part, it was. There might be an occasional article in the tabloids, but none of it really scandal. There had been talk when their sister had returned after going missing for a few years, and it had been news when Asha had been found and recognized as his brother-in-law Max's half-sister. But he'd deliberately and carefully never given the news something to talk about in the Harrison family. Not that he hadn't done anything that *could* possibly be newsworthy after his parents' deaths, but he made damn sure that the press never found out. Other than that, he'd kept his goddamn control, and he wasn't about to lose it.

Travis released a frustrated groan and put the car in gear with a little more force than necessary. He executed a precision turn, the tires squealing as he left the pavement and started down the dirt road that led to the freeway.

I'm not doing this. I'm not. I'm not going to stalk the woman like some kind of lunatic with a dick that's about to explode! I have control. I've always had control.

"Fuck it!" Travis growled, stopping the vehicle while he pulled out his cell phone, looked up the location of Sully's Oasis, and programmed the address of the bar into his navigation system. Christ! Did she have to work in *that* neighborhood? The bar wasn't far from the Hudson clinic, the same place where Simon's wife, Kara, had been attacked by drug addicts. Didn't Ally have any sense? And what the hell was wrong with her ex that he actually let her work in that area with drunken men?

Shit! It's a public place. I can just stop in for a drink.

Travis *was* doing it, and he no longer gave a shit about the repercussions.

Chapter 3

S trangely enough, although Ally loved the work she did at Harrison much more than mixing drinks, she felt the most comfortable here at Sully's. It might be a mind-numbingly boring job sometimes, but it was a place where she could be herself, and not have to be on pins and needles all night like she was in her job at Harrison. It might not be as interesting, but it was a lot more relaxed. It wasn't in the best neighborhood, but most of the customers were regulars, people she saw almost on a nightly basis because it was a small, friendly bar. And Charlie Sullivan was the fatherly type. Her boss here at Sully's was way different from her billionaire boss from Hell at Harrison. If any guy ever gave her hard time in any way, Charlie booted his ass out the door. He didn't put up with anyone harassing his bartender or cocktail waitresses.

It was getting later, and the crowd in the small bar was thinning. It was Wednesday, a typically slow night anyway. She wiped down the bar, smiling at several of the patrons she knew, making drink orders in between her cleanup.

She hadn't told anyone at Sully's about her breakup with Rick. She'd never had an engagement ring because Rick had never had the extra money, so it wasn't like Tina or any of the other ladies here at Sully's had any physical indication that anything had happened. And it was too humiliating to share the fact that her fiancé had been screwing another woman in their bed. She'd kept her problems to herself, coming to work here every evening and just doing her job.

The only person she had confided in was Travis.

"Happy Birthday, Ally!" Charlie Sullivan, a big bear of man with reddish hair and a booming voice, came out of the back room, carrying a tray of drinks.

"What's this?" Ally asked, puzzled. *Tomorrow* was her birthday, but she hardly wanted to be reminded that she was turning twenty-eight years old, and no longer had a life plan of any kind.

Her middle-aged boss patted her on the back as he brought the drinks to an empty table. "You told me just the other day that even though you make these drinks, you've never tried any of them. I think you need a little birthday surprise. Time to try out something new."

"I have to work tomorrow. And I have to drive home." She gave Charlie a dubious look. She didn't care for beer, and she did have an occasional glass of wine, but that was the limits of her experience with alcohol. Having been the only child of an alcoholic, she didn't experiment much with booze. Maybe it was a bit odd that she was a bartender and yet had never been drunk. But she never had the time to breathe, much less be laid up with a hangover.

"I'll take you home," Charlie replied, taking her by the arm and leading her around from behind the bar.

"Come on, Ally," Tina, one of the waitresses, encouraged as she sidled up to the table. "Live a little. Try a few."

"I'm not completely done with my cleanup," Ally protested laughingly as Charlie brought her over to the table.

"I'll clean up. And make any drinks that need to be served. Try out your instructor's concoctions," Charlie encouraged.

Ally looked down at the tray of drinks, and then around the bar. There were only a few regulars, and they had already crowded around the table, patting her on the back and hooting for her to celebrate her birthday.

The tray consisted of almost all Blow Jobs, a drink that she'd made about a thousand times, and watched women consume with great relish every single weekend. Charlie had piled the whipped cream on the shot glasses high, which would make it almost impossible for her not to make a mess.

Live a little.

Really, Ally had never really lived, never did one thing that wasn't carefully planned. Would it really hurt to try to have a little fun just once, laugh with a few friends? It wasn't like she was going to become an alcoholic like her mother just from having a few drinks. Tomorrow was her birthday, and she'd be spending the entire day taking shit from Travis.

Do it, Ally. For once in your life, do something spontaneous. It's a special occasion.

"Oh hell, why not?" she conceded, reaching for one of the shot glasses.

"Oh, no," Tina said laughingly, playfully slapping Ally's hand. "You have to do it the right way."

Ally groaned, but compliantly put her hands behind her back when Charlie positioned them for her. She'd just try it once. Tina put the drink on a napkin on the table.

Ally had seen this done by other women often, but they made it look much easier than it actually was. Opening her mouth wide, she felt the burst of silky sweetness hit her taste buds and closed her lips around the rim of the shot glass. Unfortunately, the drink slipped and she only downed about half of it, the rest falling down the front of her t-shirt as the glass shot out of her mouth and to the floor.

Everyone groaned, and then laughed uproariously, encouraging her to try again. Tina came forward and gave her instructions on the fine art of doing Blow Jobs, and Ally tried again, getting the entire thing down this time. It was sweet, smooth, and went down easily, the taste delicious. She licked the cream off her mouth and went for just one more.

"Ally, if you're going to do a blow job, you have to do it right. Tip your head back farther and swallow."

Travis stopped in his tracks, his whole body freezing as he heard that booming comment from outside the small bar. His hand tightened on the doorknob until his knuckles were white.

Ally? Blow jobs? Swallowing? Holy fuck, no!

Travis felt his anger rising to the surface, something that almost never happened. He rarely let it get that far before stuffing it back inside him, except for his normal disagreements with Ally. But it wasn't the same kind of anger; it was the much more dangerous kind. His stomach rolled at the thought of what he might find when he stepped inside, and he was suddenly feeling homicidal at the thought of Ally touching anyone in that way—or any way at all.

He heard several men laughing and one female voice that didn't belong to Ally. What in the hell? Were they having a bar orgy?

Travis put all of his weight against the door as he turned the knob, the forward motion propelling him into the one-room tavern. There, in the middle of the room, was Ally. There was a man holding her hands behind her back, and Ally had her head tilted backward so far Travis was surprised her neck didn't snap. One woman and several men stood around the table, all of them smiling.

Bastards!

"What in the hell are you doing?" Travis bellowed, causing Ally's head to snap forward, and a shot glass to pop out of her mouth. Judging by the amount of empty glasses already on the table, it wasn't the first.

Ally eyed him in horror, her tongue snaking out to catch white cream from her lips.

Anger was pulsating in waves from Travis as he growled, "Take your fucking hands off her or I'll break every finger you've got."

Seeing the man, any man, handling Ally made him lose control. And the fact that he was holding Ally in a submissive position nearly had him jumping on top of the guy and pounding the hell out of him.

The older man backed away from her. "Look, man, I'm not looking for a fight. Ally's my employee. We were just celebrating her birthday."

"They're all friends," Ally confirmed, licking at her lips again.

"This your guy, Ally?" the older man asked, looking toward Ally.

"No," Ally replied, moving over to Travis. "What are you doing here?" she whispered anxiously.

"I'm Travis Harrison. And she's my employee, too." Now why in the hell had he said that? He hated telling people who he was. There were very few people who wouldn't recognize the name. He looked down at Ally with a scowl. "Are you sure they weren't hurting you?"

"Totally sure," she replied, her green eyes slightly glassy.

It was the only answer that kept Travis from beating the hell out of all the men. "Are you drunk?" he asked, surprised.

She covered her mouth and hiccupped. "I think I might be a little tipsy. I don't usually drink."

"I'm taking her home. She's not driving," the older man who'd been holding Ally's hands behind her back added.

Only in your fucking dreams, man. Travis shot the auburn-haired guy a warning look. "I'm taking her home," he informed everyone, his tone daring them to argue. There was no way he was letting anybody near her right now. She was too damn vulnerable in her condition.

Ally put a hand on his arm, and he looked down into her liquid emerald eyes, and then raked her entire body with his gaze. The tank top she was wearing was thin and wet, and he could see the outline of her nipples through the skimpy, low-cut top and obviously damp bra. She had on jeans and sneakers, and he noticed for the first time that her hair was down, the mass of blonde curls tumbling over her shoulders.

"I was just doing Blow Jobs. I've never done them before. Would you like a Blow Job?" Ally asked him, licking her lips again.

Travis almost came in his jeans. Ally was definitely a little beyond tipsy, and had no idea what she was saying. There was no guile on her face, no seductive expression. She was simply offering him a drink because she was in an inebriated daze. But Christ, hearing those words from *her lips* was one of his horniest fantasies, and watching her flick her tongue to keep licking her sticky, full lips was nearly killing him.

He grabbed her hand and pulled her toward the door. "Time to go home, Alison."

"Wait." She pulled her hand from his and turned to Charlie. "Thanks, Charlie. I had…fun."

Charlie grabbed her purse from under the bar and handed it to her. "Have a good birthday, Ally," he said sincerely.

Travis grabbed her hand, watching her wave happily at the remaining people in the bar as he dragged her out the door.

"Guess you didn't want a Blow Job. They're actually really good," Ally told him cheerfully as they exited the bar.

"For Christ's sake…stop saying that, Alison." Travis tried to sound calm, tried to keep the desperation out of his voice. If she asked him about *that* one more time, his cock was definitely going to detonate.

He got her to the car and strapped her into the seat, before moving around to the driver's side. Tomorrow, they were going to have a very serious talk about her safety. Or maybe there would be no talk…just action. That was what he was good at, and he planned on making certain that Ally was okay from now on. Obviously no one else seemed to worry about her, and her dickhead fiancé had never cared.

Travis knew her parents were both dead, and that she had no siblings. Her father had died when she was very young, and her mother had passed away soon after she had started college. No wonder she had been ripe for the first asshole who had promised her forever. She'd been easy pickings for a hustler like her ex, probably still grieving and alone. Not that she had shared those things with *him*. Most of her history he'd learned from Kade, and for some reason, that completely pissed him off.

Maybe she talks to Kade because he isn't an asshole to her like I am.

Travis drove Ally home, saying very little except to get directions to her house. He was afraid that if he said *anything*, he would definitely lose control. There was no forgetting that moment when he'd seen her with her hands being held behind her back by some other guy. His protective instincts had flared, and he'd been ready to throttle the bastard just for touching Ally, even though the situation had been mostly innocent. He hadn't reasoned, hadn't thought anything through...he'd just reacted. Things didn't work that way for him, not usually. He was a planner, a thinker, weighing the risks and benefits of every action. And he never, ever did anything remotely emotional or scandalous.

"Why did you come to the bar tonight?" Ally asked quietly, sounding more lucid; clearly, the drive home had sobered her up a little. "I know it's definitely not one of your usual hangouts."

"I wanted to make sure you were doing okay," Travis answered honestly as he pulled into Ally's driveway.

"Is it because I nearly had a meltdown in your office earlier?"

No. It really wasn't. He'd done it because he hadn't been able to stay away after he'd realized exactly what her situation was in life right now. How could he explain that he suddenly wanted to protect her, fix things for her, in addition to the fact that he was dying to fuck her? He didn't even understand it himself. But he answered, "Yes." It was the easiest excuse.

"I'll be okay."

Fuck! Her voice sounded tentative and vulnerable, and Travis had all he could do not to find her ex and kill the son of a bitch. He'd screwed Ally over, and left her all alone, in a bad situation, after she'd given him everything. Didn't the asshole know just how valuable that kind of devotion was from a woman? Did he even care? "I know you'll be fine," Travis said gruffly. He planned on making damn sure she was from now on.

Ally seemed steadier as he helped her out of the car. She ran her hand lovingly over the hood of his Ferrari. "Well, it least I got to ride in one of your expensive cars," she said jokingly. "This one is beautiful."

"It isn't that expensive compared to some of my other ones at the track," he admitted. "But I like it for casual driving."

Ally's delighted laughter flowed over Travis like a balm to his soul.

"I'd kill to drive this F12, and you're talking about it like it's a cheap family car." Ally snorted.

Travis felt the edges of his mouth start to tug. "I just got a Hennessey today. I was testing it out before I came to see you."

Travis actually did smile when he heard Ally gasp as she said, "A Venom GT?"

"Yes," he answered, surprised that Ally knew so much about cars. "You know your vehicles."

"I grew up in Daytona Beach. I worked the concessions at the raceway in high school. It would have been hard not to learn something about fast cars," she answered, amused. "I still pay attention."

"I've driven that track more than once," Travis told her as he walked her to the door.

"I know," Ally answered, digging her keys out of her purse. "Do you ever regret it, giving up a professional career as a driver?"

Travis shook his head. "No. I like running Harrison. I think if racing had become my full-time profession, it wouldn't be fun anymore." Harrison Corporation was who he was, and he would never let it be put in the hands of someone else to manage it while he was out racing cars.

Travis took the keychain out of her hand when she had problems getting the key in the door. She might be less drunk, but she wasn't completely sober either. He opened the door, handing her back her keys. She'd flipped on the lights, and Travis's covetous gaze feasted on the sight of her. Her eyes were still bright, but she was looking at him intently, as though she'd never seen him before. Her gaze moved over his entire body boldly, landing on his lips with a look of longing.

"Would you kiss me?" she asked him hesitantly, her stare still intent on his lips.

Travis stared right back at her, wanting to tell her she was the most kissable, fuckable woman on the planet. He wanted to devour her mouth more than he wanted anything else in the world right at that moment. But he made himself white-knuckle the doorframe to keep himself from touching her. "You're not in your right mind, Alison. You don't know what you want right now. Take a couple of aspirin and go to bed." *Holy shit...that hurt.* Travis had nearly gagged on the words, wanting something else completely, but he was unwilling to take advantage of Ally when she'd had a few drinks. This situation made him even harder than when she'd offered him a Blow Job, probably because she kind of knew what she was asking for this time. She was asking for him.

Her gaze left his mouth and she shook her head. "I'm sorry. I don't know why I asked."

He sure as fuck hoped it was because she wanted him, even if it was just a little. "Close the door and lock it." He wasn't budging until he heard the deadbolt put in place. He needed to leave, get the hell away from her before he changed his mind.

She nodded, starting to swing the door closed, her eyes not meeting his.

"Alison?" he said quickly before she closed the door.

She paused. "Yes?"

Don't kiss her. Don't take advantage of her. You'll hate yourself later.

Travis gripped the wood a little harder. "I'll pick you up around eight in the morning and send someone to get your car." He pushed himself away from the door frame so she could close the door. "And if you're feeling okay, I'll let you drive the F12 in the morning."

"You will?" she asked, sounding shocked.

Travis shrugged. It was just a car. And there wasn't anything he wouldn't do if he could just get her to smile at him. "It's your birthday," he used as an explanation for his actions, knowing he'd let her do it anyway just because she wanted to. "Now lock up," he demanded.

Ally closed the door obediently, and the tumbler on the deadbolt flipped immediately.

Good girl.

Travis's heart was still racing as he walked back to his car, got in, and started the ignition. He leaned his head against the steering wheel for a moment, trying to catch his breath. *Jesus!* Not touching Ally tonight had been the hardest thing he'd ever done. He wanted her badly, but not that way. He needed her warm and willing, aware of everything that was happening. And maybe there was a small part of him that didn't want her to have any regrets, didn't want her to hate him because he took advantage. His instinct to protect her was just as strong as his desire to fuck her, and that was saying a hell of a lot, because that yearning was damn near killing him.

He already knew what his dreams would look like tonight. There was no way he wouldn't be dreaming vividly about Ally asking him if he wanted a blow job, licking those luscious lips as she uttered the words every man in the world wanted to hear from a woman he wanted. And in his dreams, Travis would never refuse to kiss her. Hell, he'd probably have a damn heart attack and die in his sleep when he answered her differently, did exactly what he'd wanted to do earlier when she uttered those requests in his dreams tonight.

Travis waited until the lights went on upstairs before he backed out of the driveway and drove away, wondering when in the hell he'd actually developed a conscience, and hating himself because when it came to Ally…he actually had one.

Chapter 4

Ally woke up late the next morning, with barely thirty minutes to get ready for work. She hadn't wanted to drag her butt out of bed, and she wasn't certain whether it was really the alcohol she'd consumed the night before, or the fact that she was going to have to face Travis.

Oh God, did I really ask him to kiss me?

She frowned at herself in the mirror as she hastily gathered her hair into a clip at the back of her head, in too much of a hurry to worry about braiding or a more intricate style. She'd only put on a minimal amount of makeup, just enough so she didn't scare any of Harrison Corporation's clients.

Running to her closet to grab a pair of shoes and a colorful belt to match the conservative gray dress she had thrown on earlier, she looked nervously at the clock.

Five minutes until eight o'clock.

Ally had no doubt that Travis would arrive at exactly eight, ready to leave for the office. He didn't have any early morning appointments, but she could tell the time by Travis's arrival in the morning. Travis Harrison was never late, and he arrived at exactly the same time every single day.

"Shit," Ally cursed as the closet door caught her nylons, starting a snag that turned into a very long run in her panty hose. She watched as she turned her leg to look at it, irritated as she watched it go from her knee to her ankle. Snatching her black heels, she dropped them on the floor and fastened the black, gray, and red belt around her waist, adding some color to the drab dress. At least she could breathe in the ugly dress. It had a fuller skirt to accommodate her curvy hips.

Rifling through her dresser drawer, desperate to find another pair of black hose, the only thing she came up with was an ultra-thin pair of stockings and a black garter belt. "Crap," she said, annoyed with herself for not stocking up again on panty hose. She eyed the sexy black ensemble warily, having dug to the bottom of her drawer to uncover it. She'd bought it on a whim a few years ago, and had only worn it once, when she and Rick were supposedly going out for a romantic evening to celebrate Valentine's Day. Unfortunately, Rick had called her to cancel, claiming he had to study. She'd undressed and went to bed, washing the lingerie and never bothering to wear it again, feeling more than a little bit silly for trying to spice up their sex life. Rick had been too busy, too tired all the time. Now, Ally had to wonder if her ex-fiancé had been full of shit, even then. Just that thought made Ally want to trash the lingerie, but she was desperate, so she quickly put on the stockings, garter belt, and the sexy black panties that went with the set. It didn't matter. They were black stockings, and nobody would ever know that they were attached to a *fuck-me* set of lingerie.

Ally cringed as she heard the doorbell ring, putting her heels on carefully so she didn't snag the last pair of stockings she had. "How in the hell am I going to look him in the eye after asking him to kiss me? Maybe he won't say anything. He knew I'd had a few drinks," she whispered to herself hopefully.

Actually, she hadn't been drunk when she'd asked Travis to kiss her. The alcohol had lessened her inhibitions, but she'd desperately wanted to feel what it would be like to have that sinful mouth of his on hers. Asking him to kiss her was possibly *the* most impetuous thing she'd ever done. He was her boss, for God's sake, and a man who could have any woman he wanted. Still, those important facts hadn't stopped her longing to see what his kiss would feel like just once. Ever since Travis had told her how desirable she was, Ally had wanted to see if his kiss backed up his words. Knowing Travis, he'd probably act like he didn't remember, or maybe it wouldn't even be important enough for him to recall.

She raced down the stairs as fast as her heels would allow, breathless by the time she opened the door. Travis looked immaculate as usual, but his stance was casual, his hands in the pockets of his suit pants. Ally's breath caught as she took in his black designer suit, the only relief from the darkness of the outfit some small navy and gray stripes on his tie.

"Good morning, Ms. Caldwell," Travis said huskily. "I trust you're recovered?" His dark eyes perused her thoroughly, as though looking for any signs of a hangover.

"I-I'm fine," Ally answered nervously, opening the door wider so he could enter, hating herself for being anxious. She couldn't show any weaknesses to Travis. The man was like a shark that could scent blood in the water. If he knew he had her rattled, he'd swoop in for the kill. It was a trait that made him a good businessman, but a dangerous adversary. "Let me grab my purse and a cup of coffee to take with me. Would you like one?"

Travis sauntered into the living room, and Ally closed the door behind him.

"I'm not in any hurry," Travis said casually. "Take your time."

Ally looked at Travis, dumbfounded. Since when *wasn't* he in a hurry? The man never wasted a single moment, working like a fiend every moment of the day. She turned, slightly confused, and walked into the kitchen, her heels clicking against the polished wood of the floor as she took down two mugs and poured the coffee that she'd set up to brew on a timer the night before. Quickly adding creamer to her coffee, she left Travis's black the way he liked it, and headed quickly back to the living room. Travis had his back to her, looking at her bookshelves that lined an entire wall in her living room. She'd been planning on moving most of them into one of the spare rooms to use as a library, but she hadn't bothered. She'd be moving soon anyway. "Here you go." Ally handed him his mug carefully.

Travis turned to her and raised a brow. "You do realize, Ms. Caldwell, that you actually brought me my coffee today."

"Don't get used to it," she mumbled over the rim of her coffee before taking a careful sip.

Travis smirked as he said, "You have eclectic reading tastes. I think you have everything from the classics to non-fiction to do-it-yourself books here."

Ally shrugged uncomfortably. "I like to read."

"What's this?" Travis asked curiously, pulling out a plain, bound manuscript.

She leaped forward, trying to pull the bound sheets from his fingers. "Nothing of interest," she told him adamantly. "Give it to me."

"It has your name on it. Did you write it?" There was no scorn in his voice, only curiosity, as he held the manuscript out of her reach.

"Yes," Ally answered irritably.

Setting his coffee down on one of the shelves, he flipped through the pages. "You're a writer?"

"I'm an assistant and a secretary. And I'm a bartender. Writing was just a dream."

"Why?" Travis's gaze locked with hers, his dark eyes questioning.

"Because I wasn't good enough to be published. I have the rejection letters to prove it," she answered, annoyed. "Rick told me to quit dreaming and work harder at something that actually paid a wage. And he was right. We were tight on money. I needed an extra job where I actually got paid—"

"Is this a fantasy novel?" Travis interrupted, his concentration on the manuscript.

"Yes," Ally admitted. "Young adult fantasy. It's a series. I never quite finished the second book." Not that she wasn't itching to write the story, but there was just never a moment where she had the time to write. Someday she *would* finish the series, even if she couldn't get it published.

"I'd like to read it," Travis said thoughtfully, closing the manuscript gently and placing it next to his coffee. "So the bastard basically took everything away from you," Travis stated quietly, his voice low and dangerous.

"What do you mean?" Ally asked, confused.

Travis crossed his arms in front of him and his brows narrowed, spearing Ally with a dark glare. "He made you quit school so he could finish. Then he made you give up your writing to work even more hours at a goddamn bar in a shitty neighborhood. He shamed you into doing exactly what he needed. Did he ever give a damn about you, what you wanted? Obviously not, or he wouldn't have been hopping into another woman's bed."

Ally opened her mouth, wanting to tell him that Rick hadn't technically hopped into another woman's bed. He'd used theirs. But she wasn't so sure her slimy ex hadn't done some hopping, too. "It wasn't all him," she admitted reluctantly. "I wanted security, too. That was the plan. To finally have a life that wasn't chaos, a life where I didn't have to worry about pinching every single penny I had."

"And was your life always so chaotic?" Travis asked as he stepped forward, stopping a few feet away from her.

"Yes. I grew up with one parent, and she was an alcoholic, drunk more often than she was sober. So yes, I wanted a normal life." Ally's heart was racing, and she took a deep breath and let it out. It wasn't that she didn't know that she was a codependent mess sometimes, but it wasn't a topic she really wanted to discuss with someone like Travis. Actually, she didn't really discuss it with anyone.

"So you busted your ass to make the wrong guy happy, a man who didn't give a shit about what actually made you happy," Travis stated flatly. "So when is it your turn, Ms. Caldwell?"

"I'll have my chance as soon as I straighten everything out," Ally argued.

"Will you? I wonder?" Travis said hoarsely.

"I can't change the past. Yes…I was stupid. Yes…I was gullible. I need to learn from my mistakes and move on," Ally said hesitantly.

"You're a pragmatic organizer on the surface, but a dreamer inside," Travis observed. "But one thing I don't understand is why you took his shit for so long. You're not the type of woman to put up with crap from anyone. I should know. He must have been one hell of a manipulator."

Ally shifted uncomfortably. "He was." Rick was never openly hostile or angry. Ally could have dealt with that by kneeing him in the balls and walking away. But he had a way of making her feel guilty and responsible for everything, and he'd played on her vulnerabilities. "He was very good at it." Ally sighed. "I guess I wanted the dream, and I had everything planned out perfectly. It just didn't work out exactly the way I had planned." She'd dealt with everything Rick threw at her just for the possibility that some day she might have a normal life, making excuses for him just like she'd made excuses for her alcoholic mother all her life. She told herself life would get better, that Rick would be a better man once he wasn't under so much stress. It wasn't until the moment she'd seen him screwing another woman that she realized that she'd been the one living a lie. He'd always been an asshole. Seeing him with another woman had finally shaken her into reality.

"You're a smart woman, smart enough to get anything you want," Travis said huskily, stepping close enough to tuck a loose strand of hair behind her ear. "Did you love him?"

Ally glanced up at Travis, their gazes locking together, and she was unable to look away. His expression was stoic, but his eyes were heated with a mesmerizing stare that made every thought except him fly out her brain. "I-I don't think I ever knew him. I think I loved the idea of a plan and a normal life." Travis was close enough to smell now, and Ally stepped back for her own self-protection, her back hitting the living room wall. She'd already made an ass of herself the night before. Travis was her boss, the billionaire boss from Hell, and she needed to remember exactly who he was. For some reason, she had memory problems when he got this close, like everything in her body overheated and short-circuited.

Travis moved forward and braced one hand against the wall beside her head, the index finger of his other hand moving in a pattern from her ear to her cheek. "Ask me to kiss you again, Alison," he demanded, his finger tracing her lips.

Ally wanted to break eye contact, wanted to run as fast and far away from Travis as she could possibly get. The grim expression on his face was at odds with the torridity of his dark, liquid eyes: a look that both frightened and enthralled her.

She didn't want to think about his rejection the night before, or why he wanted her to ask again. Finally, she simply asked, "Why?"

Travis took the coffee from her hand and set it on a small table next to him, his eyes never leaving her as he tipped her chin up, his thumb stroking over her skin as he answered, "Because I've been waiting all night for you to ask me again, this time when you're sober. Ask me," he rasped demandingly, his breath moving in and out of his lungs as though he'd just finished a long, hard run.

Oh, how Ally wanted to heed this one command from Travis. She wanted to feel those hard, demanding lips on hers more than she wanted her next breath. But she whispered, "I can't. You're my boss. I'm your employee. We can't do this."

"The hell we can't. You're fired," he grumbled.

Maybe this was the one time that Ally appreciated the fact that Travis canned her on a daily basis. "Fine," she answered, grasping his dark, immaculate tie and yanking his mouth down to hers, unable to overcome the temptation to touch him, have him touch her. Her eyes slid closed, her senses immediately intoxicated by the feel of his hot, demanding mouth covering hers, his insistent tongue overcoming any resistance or hesitance she may have had earlier. She opened to him, and he plundered, taking what he wanted, and at the same time giving her exactly what she needed.

Ally moaned into his kiss, her hands spearing into his coarse, dark hair, shivering at the feel of the strands sifting between her fingers. He palmed her ass with one hand, brought her up hard against his muscular, heated body. His fingers grasped the clip in her hair and pulled, releasing a cascade of blonde locks down her back. Fisting her hair, he tilted her head back further, allowing him complete access to her mouth.

Sweet Jesus, I'm in trouble!

Travis kissed like a man possessed, and Ally responded, giving back exactly what he gave to her, lust crashing over her body like a tidal wave. Her core flooded with liquid heat, and she rubbed her body against him in frustrated passion, irritated because she needed to feel his heated skin against hers. His heavy suit jacket kept her hands from touching his bare skin, and she wanted it gone. She wanted everything gone.

Travis tore his mouth from hers, panting. Another tug on her hair bared the sensitive skin of her neck, and his mouth explored, as though savoring every exposed surface of her body. "If you don't stop rubbing that luscious body against me, I'll have you naked and on your back within seconds," he warned her ominously, his low voice muffled against her temple. "Or naked up against the wall," he added harshly.

For one crazy, wild moment, Ally wanted to call Travis's bluff, press herself against the large erection she could already feel against her lower abdomen. But she felt too raw, too exposed. And leaving herself open to Travis would be just another stupid mistake. He was too dark, too tempting, and far too unpredictable. The last thing she needed was to have a fling with her boss and lose her job. As much as she wanted him—and she definitely did—she was terrified of what the outcome of an affair with Travis would be. He was a heartless prick. Maybe he felt like playing with her now, but he'd find another toy soon enough. And she'd be out of a job.

"We'll be late for work." Ally tried not to whimper.

"I own the company. I don't think we'll get in trouble," Travis answered lazily, nipping at her earlobe.

Dear Lord, if she didn't get away from him now, she *would* tear his clothes off. He pulled his head back to give her a scorching look, one that almost had her stripping him right there. His hair was mussed, like he'd just rolled out of bed—or gotten screwed—and his clothing was askew. It was a whole new look on her boss, and damn, it looked really good on him. It made him seem more approachable, and even sexier than he normally looked. "I forgot. I don't have a job. You fired me." She tugged playfully on his hair.

"I could think of a few things that would probably persuade me to re-hire you," Travis answered in a graveled voice, his hand tightening on her ass possessively.

Unable to handle the exquisite torture of Travis's touch for a moment longer, Ally ducked under his arm and scooted away from him. "We shouldn't have done that," she said unhappily.

Travis straightened his tie and smoothed his hair back down. "It was just a kiss, Alison." His eyes shuttered and his face turned to his usual, stony expression.

Just a kiss? Bastard!

His tone was mocking, irritating, and she wanted to slap him for calling what they'd just done simply a kiss. For her, it had been an earth-shattering, panty-melting experience, an embrace that still had her body melting from the heat.

Without another word, she picked up her purse, turning her back on him. "Right. Just a kiss. Nothing spectacular," she answered nonchalantly, hoping none of the hurt she felt could be detected in her voice. Really, did she even know what a normal hot kiss was like? Maybe it really *wasn't* anything extraordinary. She had very little to compare it with.

She turned in time to see Travis picking up her manuscript and slugging the last of his coffee. For a moment, she considered arguing with him about taking her book, but she wrote so people could read the stories she had to share, therefore it really didn't matter. He moved to take the mug to the kitchen, but she intercepted it and dropped both cups off in the sink herself. Picking up her hair clip from the floor, she scraped her hair back and tightened the clasp. "Time to go," she said, breezing through the living room to the door, hoping she sounded calmer than she felt.

Travis caught up with her at the door, grasping her upper arm as she opened the door. "He was a fool to lose you, Alison," he said gruffly. "And if I thought you were ready and wouldn't regret it, I'd be fucking you right now. Watching you come would be one of the most satisfying things I've ever done."

Ally gaped at him for a moment, stunned at how fiery he could be at one moment, and then turn to ice the next. Her face flushed, and she could feel the sensual electricity flow between them, knowing that one misplaced spark would fire a roaring flame. "I doubt that. And it was just a kiss," she reminded him with false sweetness in her voice.

"It was more than that," he admitted, his eyes raking over her face, searching for…something.

Ally turned away, unable to withstand his scrutiny. She'd exposed too much of herself already. Opening the door, she waited for him to step through before locking up behind him. As she turned around, she saw that he was dangling a set of keys in front of her face.

"I did promise," he said, sounding almost pained.

Ally swiped the keys. "I promise I'll get us to Harrison without a scratch on the car."

Travis shrugged. "It's not the car I'm concerned about."

He helped her into the driver's seat and buckled her in, and then took his own seat on the other side. "You're not used to the vehicle."

Travis proceeded to give her clipped instructions all the way to work, even though Ally handled the car just fine. She may not have ever driven a Ferrari, but she understood all the car had to offer. Occasionally, she accelerated too fast, causing Travis to snarl at her to slow down. When she finally pulled the sports car into Travis's personal parking space, he grudgingly admitted she had driven well, but spoiled the compliment by reminding her that she drove too fast. Like she was going to drive a Ferrari like a grandma? Had Travis not been snapping at her for her speed, she would have liked to open the engine up a little more, although there were few places where she could do that in the city. Still, the experience had been exhilarating.

"Thank you," she told him sincerely as she handed back his keys outside the Harrison building. "You just helped me complete one thing on my bucket list."

"I hardly think turning twenty-eight requires a bucket list, Alison," Travis replied, straightening his tie as they walked into the building.

Ally shrugged as they stepped into the elevator. "You never know. I might get the death penalty after I kill my billionaire boss from Hell," she answered smoothly, shooting him an evil smile. "Do you have your phone?"

Travis scowled at her. "Yes. Why?"

"I just wanted to add some reminders." She was such a liar, but whenever he started to act like he had a stick up his butt, she had wicked thoughts.

He handed it over with a masculine sigh. "If you change the ringtone, you're fired."

"Would I do that?" She put a hand to her chest, giving a false look of horror and dismay.

Travis glared at her. "Yes," he growled.

Ally did put in a few reminders as they stood in the elevator.

And then she changed his ringtone to a popular and very sexually explicit song, making sure the volume was full blast.

She smiled at him innocently as she handed it back, reminding herself to call him during one of his meetings today. With that supremely satisfying thought in mind, she stepped out of the elevator and made her way into the office, her grin broadening with every step she took.

Chapter 5

"You're fired!" Ally had to hold the cell phone away from her ear to diminish the sound of Travis's booming voice. "I was in a meeting with a bunch of very uptight old men when you called me. I thought they were all going to have a heart attack."

Ally stifled a laugh as she put the phone back to her ear. "I'm sorry, Mr. Harrison, but I'm on my lunch right now. Feel free to berate me as soon as I get back to the office and I'm on the clock again." She clicked the Off button on the phone, cutting off what she was certain would have been another long lecture from Travis. "He fired me." Ally sighed and smiled wickedly at Asha Harrison. She and Asha had become friends since Asha had married Kade, the two of them getting together as often as they could.

Today, Asha had brought her a bouquet of flowers for her birthday, and insisted on taking her out for lunch. They were currently seated in a casual Italian restaurant, devouring sinful plates of pasta.

Asha looked radiantly pregnant and happy, and that fact made Ally genuinely smile. After all that Asha had been through, she deserved the happiness she'd found with Kade. Unlike Travis, Kade was a very likable man, and almost the complete opposite of his twin.

While Travis was dark in both appearance and personality, Kade was blond and gorgeous, a former pro football player who almost always seemed to be wearing a grin, especially since he'd married Asha.

"You know…it isn't like Travis couldn't just check his phone and turn off any ringtone you set," Asha mused, wiping her mouth with her napkin. "He's a brilliant man, smart enough to think of doing that every day."

Ally had often contemplated the same question. "I think he likes a reason to fight. He's obstinate that way," she replied, taking a sip of water to wash down the pasta.

So much for my diet. I might as well take the fettuccini and apply it directly to my hips.

"I think he does it on purpose," Asha replied. "So he has a reason to seek you out."

Ally snorted. "I doubt that. He avoids me like the plague. He's been a bit…different. He's only been a little less of an asshole since I broke up with my fiancé." She'd told Asha about her breakup on the way to the restaurant.

And now he's taken to kissing me breathless! Ally decided not to share that little fact with Asha. More than likely it would get back to Kade.

"How different?" Asha questioned curiously.

Ally shrugged. "He listens occasionally. And he let me drive his Ferrari today because it was my birthday."

Asha let out a low whistle. "That's major," she said sincerely. "He rarely even lets Kade drive his vehicles." She put her fork down on her plate and picked up her water. "I think he has the hots for you. And so does my handsome husband."

Ally nearly choked on her water, swallowing it with difficulty. She actually flushed when she thought about the heated kiss Travis had laid on her that morning. "I'm his assistant, and I irritate the hell out of him. I doubt very much that he's lusting after me," Ally denied, giving Asha a dubious look. He might have kissed her, and maybe he really would screw her, but Ally suspected it was just because she was single now, convenient and available.

"I've watched him when you're around. He's lusting," Asha stated adamantly. "And neither of the Harrison men have ever been players. Kade had a longtime girlfriend to whom he was faithful for years, even though the bitch dropped him the moment he wasn't physically perfect anymore. And Kade said that Travis is never seen with a woman. He had a few brief relationships in college, but nothing much since then."

Asha was right. Travis *did* do everything alone. "Are you trying to tell me that Travis Harrison never gets laid?" she asked Asha curiously.

"If he does, he's quiet about it," Asha replied thoughtfully. "Travis likes to play the badass, but he does have a heart. He's done some wonderful things with his charities."

"I know," Ally admitted. "If he wasn't such a jackass, I'd probably worship him because he's a brilliant businessman and humanitarian."

"I think since he's the oldest, he feels totally responsible for repairing the Harrison name after the scandal with his parents. The whole family was completely humiliated, and hounded unmercifully by the press. Their life was a living hell for a very long time."

Although Ally hadn't known Travis at that time, she knew about the Harrison scandal; she knew that the siblings' father had killed their mother and then took his own life. "It had to have been horrible for all of them," Ally admitted, her heart bleeding for a younger and more vulnerable Travis.

Asha nodded. "It was. And Kade says Travis always got the worst of it from his father because he was always trying to protect them. " Asha visibly shuddered. "The man was completely insane, and I can only imagine the kind of abuse Travis suffered. I know what Kade went through, but he swears that Travis took most of it."

Ally's heart squeezed in her chest. The thought of a very young Travis taking abuse from his father made her clench her fist in indignation. She'd had a chaotic upbringing and a humiliating one, but she suspected her sad childhood with her alcoholic mother had probably been nothing compared to what Travis had suffered at the hands of a madman. "What about their mother?"

Asha hesitated for moment before answering. "I don't know, but from what Kade has told me, I'm not sure she was all there either. She was terrified of her husband, and did nothing to protect the kids."

"So they were all completely screwed," Ally mused aloud.

"Speaking of getting screwed, how are you holding up after what happened with your lowlife fiancé?" Asha asked in a hushed tone. "Are you really okay, Ally?"

Ally nodded at Asha as she toyed with her pasta. "I am. I have some things to clear up, but I'll survive."

"I hope karma bites him in the ass," Asha said venomously. "You'd tell me if you needed anything, right?"

Ally probably wouldn't, because she rarely asked for anything from anyone, but to make Asha feel better, she answered, "Yes. I'm okay. I just need to clean up the mess and move on. Some of it's my fault. I was so blinded by my plans and what I wanted for our future that I never saw the signs that he was a snake."

"I'm so sorry you were hurt, Ally. But I'm glad you didn't marry him. Since you're on vacation next week, do you want to meet up with Maddie, Mia, Kara and me? We do lunch once a week. It's a lot of fun. We all complain about what protective pain in the asses our husbands are, and then we sigh over the sweet things they do." Asha laughed softly. "But we could focus more on the man-bashing for you."

Ally laughed. "I'd like that. I haven't had much time for friends in the last few years." She hadn't had any time, but she wanted to. Although she wasn't as well acquainted with the other women, she liked them all. Sliding out of her seat, she grabbed up her purse to take out some money for her lunch. "I suppose I should get back to the office so Travis can give me his daily lecture and hire me back again."

Asha got to her feet and grasped Ally's wrist. "My treat. It's your birthday." Asha handed the waiter the small folder filled with cash.

"Thanks, Asha. And thank Kade for the flowers in case I don't see him today. They're beautiful." She hugged the slender Indian woman, grateful that the two of them had become friends.

"I have no doubt you can handle Travis. You always do. I think you're the only one who can," Asha replied, squeezing Ally before letting her go.

Ally wanted to tell Asha that her skills at handling Travis were a little off lately, ever since he'd thrown her off-balance with his odd behavior and panty-melting kisses. But she simply bade her friend good-bye, agreeing to call her about lunch the following week, and drove back to the Harrison building.

She breathed a sigh of relief as she entered the office and found Travis gone, apparently out at meetings for the rest of the day according to the brief note he'd left for her. She was grateful for the reprieve, and tried to deny to herself that she was also slightly disappointed. How sick was that? She actually missed getting one of his lectures?

The afternoon flew by quickly. With Travis out of the office, she had to deal with whatever calls that she could handle, plus finish a mountain of paperwork that needed to get done. Before she knew it, she looked up at the clock and it was past time for her to leave.

I need to get to Sully's!

Quickly shutting down her computer, she opened the large bottom drawer of her desk and pulled out some spare clothing she now left at the office just in case she forgot her casual clothes for bartending. Snatching a red tank top, jeans, and her sneakers, she hesitated a moment before dashing into Travis's office and closing the door. She could be changed in a minute, and she didn't want to go down the hall to the restroom because she was short on time. The blinds were open, but the office was so far up that nobody could see her unless they were in the next building, and even then, they'd probably need binoculars.

She toed her heels off and quickly stripped off her dress, pulling the tank top over her head. She was just reaching for her jeans when Travis's office door opened, taking about ten years off her life as she let out a horrified screech.

And then…there was complete silence.

Ally froze, her gaze on Travis, his hand still on the door handle as he stared at her, his hungry eyes roaming over her body. She'd planned on covering up the sexy lingerie she was wearing with her jeans, and pulling her sneakers on over the stockings. Thinking about the image he was seeing right at that moment, she blushed, her whole face burning with embarrassment. The only thing she was wearing was a tight, red tank top, the sexy "barely there" black panties, and a matching garter belt and stockings. And with her full hips, she was fairly certain she didn't exactly look like a sex kitten. "I'm sorry. I had to change and I didn't think you were coming back."

The tension was palpable, and Travis made no attempt to leave. He just stood there in his immaculate suit and tie, his face unreadable, nearly burning her with the heat in his eyes.

Uncomfortable, Ally reached for her jeans again.

"Don't," Travis barked, closing the door behind him. He stalked toward her, his dark eyes never leaving her, almost as if he were afraid she'd bolt.

Ally couldn't move, couldn't speak, couldn't do anything except watch him as he moved slowly and deliberately across the room. Travis was stalking her, and it was the hottest thing she'd ever seen, but also a little more than terrifying. He was dangerous when he was like this, unpredictable. She could handle the Travis who was a jackass, the boss who argued with her daily. But this man, this darkly compelling and beautiful male who stopped in front of her, his eyes still roaming hungrily over her scantily clad body, was possibly more than she could handle.

He reached for the clip in her hair and released the curls as he growled, "Did he see you like this? Did you wear this for him?"

Ally swallowed before replying. She knew what Travis was asking. "No. It was an impulse buy, something he never saw and the only ones I have. I don't usually wear these. I was out of panty hose," she rambled nervously.

"Good. You're beautiful, Alison," he rumbled, thrusting a hand into her curls and fisting her hair. "I can't stomach the thought of anyone seeing you this way except me."

Ally shivered, but not with the cold. Travis's eyes turned a dark chocolate color, nearly black, and his fierceness turned her on in a way she'd never experienced before. "I'm sorry I used your office. I have to go." God, she was both weak with desire and mortified at the same time. She reached for her jeans again, but Travis caught her by the wrist, stopping her.

"Fuck! I can't let you go. Not now." Travis's voice was tormented. He used his body to back her up against his massive desk, one hand on her ass and the other still clutching her hair. "Seeing you like this makes me crazy. The only thing I want when I look at you right now is to watch you come."

Ally gulped as she stared into his eyes, as though they were having a private battle, and Travis was winning. Her treacherous body responded to his words, his nearness, and she wasn't sure she could deny him this time. The air between them was vibrating with tension, and her body was screaming from the unbearable ache to have a piece of this man, even if it was only a fling. Just for a small stolen length of time, Ally wanted to…feel. Travis wanted her. He'd made that very clear. And God, how she wanted him.

Travis lightened his hold on her hair, his fingers smoothing out the tangled strands. "Tell me that you don't want this, Alison." His voice was tense, harsh. He was challenging her even as his big body crowded her against the desk.

Ally shook her head. "I can't tell you that. But I guarantee we'll regret it later." They worked together. He was her boss. It would make their rocky working relationship even more awkward. But none of that really seemed to matter as Ally's nipples hardened to painful peaks when Travis wrapped his arm around her waist and brought her body up hard against him.

"The hell we will," Travis rumbled against her lips as his mouth came down on hers. He brought everything on his desk bar the computer to a noisy collision and then to a fall to the carpeted floor with one swipe of his powerful arm behind her. His hands went to her ass as he lifted her onto the desk, giving him better access to her mouth. He groaned against her lips, his hands pushing under her flimsy tank top to touch her bare skin.

Ally wrapped her arms around his neck, reveling in the feel of the coarse hair between her fingers as she speared her hands into his hair. Intoxicated by the masterful strokes of Travis's tongue, she shivered and opened wider to him, giving him the access he was ruthlessly demanding. He slid one hand under her hair, stroking the back of her neck, the action both sensual and dominant as he held her head in place for his rough possession.

She whimpered into his mouth as he caressed the skin of her abdomen, and then yanked her bra up and let her breast spill into his hand. He wasn't gentle, but the last thing Ally wanted was tenderness right now. Her body was on fire, her core flooded with heat and clenching with need. Travis's touch was what she needed: hard, hot, and unrelenting. And he gave it to her. He pinched and stroked, first one nipple and then the other, repeating the action while plundering her mouth until the tension in Ally's body was nearly making her insane.

He ripped his mouth from hers, his breath coming in heavy pants. Ally was just as breathless and she let her head fall back, giving him access to the sensitive skin at her neck as he explored it with his tongue, his whiskered jaw abrasive against her cheek. She closed her eyes, every nerve in her body pulsating, electrified. "Please," she hissed, begging Travis to end her torment.

"Tell me you want me," Travis commanded, his warm breath caressing her ear.

"Please," she repeated, unable to say anything else.

Travis reached up and grasped her arms, tilting her back until she was lying sprawled out on his desk. "You look like a fucking wet dream," he growled, his eyes wild and feral.

Their eyes caught and held as Travis leaned forward, his forearms resting on both sides of her. For Ally, it was like time stopped completely for just an instant, and she could see her own passion reflected in Travis's liquid, dark eyes.

He broke the stare as his head lowered to her breasts, his hands cupping and stroking her nipples before he sucked, biting down gently on one of the sensitive peaks. The pain and pleasure of it nearly broke her, her body thrashing beneath him with unsated desire.

Reaching between their bodies, Travis released her nipple and slipped his fingers beneath her delicate panties, his touch meeting nothing but liquid warmth.

"Fuck! You're so wet, and so damn hot," Travis grunted in a strangled voice. His hand fisted the fragile panties and ripped them from her body with one hard yank, the fabric tearing away from her and dropping to the floor as Travis released them, his hand returning to her bared pussy. "I can smell your arousal. You want me. You want this." He parted her thighs wide, his index finger toying mercilessly with her clit, moving over the wet bundle of nerves effortlessly.

Ally closed her eyes and moaned. "Yes." She didn't just want it; she needed it. Her entire body was rigid, coiled tightly and ready to unravel.

He used his other hand to bury one finger into her channel. "Jesus, you're tight." He eased another finger into her, moving them inside her until Ally was squirming. Travis seemed to know exactly where to touch, how to chafe against those sensitive areas inside her that made her ready to beg for relief from the torment.

Her hips lifted, needing more. "More. Please." She lifted her hands over her head and gripped the edge of the desk until she was white-knuckled, her needy moans echoing against the office walls.

His fingers thrust into her harder, faster, while he continued to caress through her smooth folds, moving more and more roughly over her clit. "Tell me what you want," he demanded coarsely. "Say my name. Tell me who you want to make you come."

"Yes, please. Make me come." Ally was out of her mind with desire, her head thrashing against the desk as her legs trembled and something tight and hot spiraled in her belly.

"Who?" He thrust into her deeply, lowering his head to bite the soft skin that was exposed on her thigh above the stockings, as though he wanted to leave his mark.

"Oh, God. Yes." His bite wasn't gentle. It was just enough to take Ally spiraling over the edge of sensation. "Travis," she finally moaned, her body trembling as her climax hit her full force.

"Come for me. I want to watch you," Travis commanded as he straightened, his gaze fixated on her face, his touch and the strokes of his fingers firm and uncompromising.

"Travis," she screamed, her being splintering apart, her entire body quivering with her explosive release.

"Look at me," he ordered, intentionally lengthening her orgasm by keeping up his assault on her sensitive clit.

Ally opened her eyes, breathless, her unfocused gaze meeting his fierce stare as her body still rippled with waves of ecstasy. "Travis?" she panted, suddenly feeling very raw and very vulnerable. Her body had never reacted this way before, and it was a little daunting to realize just how much need and passion this man could wring out of her. And he hadn't even taken off his clothes.

He pulled her up gently, wrapping his arms around her and holding her tightly against his body, as if he knew how she was feeling and he was trying to soothe her. "I was right. Watching you come is the most satisfying thing I've ever seen," Travis said huskily in her ear as he nuzzled the side of her face.

Ally took a deep breath and let it out slowly. She let her hand slide down to the front of his trousers and gently cupped the hard, sizable erection she could feel beneath the fine material. "I want to feel you inside me," she admitted in a tremulous voice.

"Don't." He grabbed her hand and brought it around his neck. "I have no control right now and I don't have a condom. I don't exactly carry one around with me just in case I get the chance to fulfill a fantasy with my assistant on my desk."

"I'm on the Pill. And I'm clean. I checked just to make sure after I broke up with Rick." Her desperation for Travis was showing, and she hated it, but she couldn't help wanting to assuage the throbbing need to have him deep inside her.

"I'm clean, too. And if you say one more word to convince me that I have no reason not to fuck you right now, I'll have you bent over this desk in a heartbeat," Travis warned her in a feral voice. "And we'll be here until morning."

Ally came out of her daze with a flash of reality. "Morning? Oh, God. I have to go to work. I'm late." She pulled away from Travis reluctantly, instantly missing the shelter of his warm body. Sully's had completely faded from her brain while she was in the midst of the most incredible climax she'd ever had.

She quickly righted her top, pulling her bra down and jerking down the tank top. Grabbing her jeans, she pulled them on, scowling at her torn panties on the floor. She bent to pick them up, but Travis beat her to it, scooping up the tattered material and shoving it into the pocket of his suit jacket. "You don't have to go," he said flatly.

"I do. It's my job," she argued, retrieving her hair clip from the floor.

"You don't. You don't work there anymore," Travis told her in a graveled voice.

Ally gaped at Travis, wondering if he'd had a few drinks before coming back to the office, but she hadn't smelled alcohol. "I don't understand."

"You've been terminated," he explained patiently, his face once again calm, his eyes icy.

Understanding dawned slowly. "You got me fired?" Ally asked, confused.

Travis leaned one hip against the desk and crossed his arms. "I wouldn't say that exactly. You were technically laid off. I had a little discussion with Mr. Sullivan before I came back to the office."

Ally felt anger rise inside her, a rage so explosive that her body started to shake. "How did you get him to agree? Did you threaten him?"

"Didn't need to do that. Money always works," Travis answered coolly.

"How can you do that to me? You knew I needed that job." Ally hated herself for ever confiding in Travis. He'd used whatever she'd told him against her. "What did I ever do to you to make you do something like this? That's my livelihood, my survival."

"This job is your survival," Travis contradicted. "And it's demanding enough. I want you freed up in case I need you."

The cold look on his face, and his casual dismissal of what he had done, set her off, and at that moment, Ally completely lost it.

Chapter 6

"You haven't needed me in four goddamn years. Why this sudden requirement?" She glared at him. "You can't just play with people's lives, Mr. Harrison. I'm not a toy. I'm a living, breathing person who needs that income right now." She stepped up to him and poked a finger in his chest, her face flushed with fury.

"No you don't," Travis answered with a smirk. "And I think I liked it better when you called me Travis."

She was quite sure he did because she'd actually been moaning his name in ecstasy. Ally exploded. "You bastard! You *are* a self-centered, egotistical prick." Tears filled her eyes, the result of the burning anger spreading through her entire being. She'd just been intimate with this man, the same man who had gotten her fired from a job that she needed right now just because it was more convenient for *him*. She lifted her hand and let it fly, the satisfying *crack* of her palm against his cheek not nearly enough to appease the hurt of his betrayal. She'd confided in him about her life in a moment of weakness, and he'd used that information to get rid of anything that might inconvenience him. "Now I don't have *any* job anymore, because I quit. You don't have to fire me this time. I can't work for you anymore. You're just another man who can't be trusted."

With as much dignity as she could possibly muster with tears streaming down her face, Ally picked up both pairs of her shoes and her dress and stormed out of Travis's office, shoving the clip for her hair into the pocket of her jeans. She gathered up her purse, leaving everything on her desk behind. She just wanted to get away from here. Asha would help her by retrieving the rest of her things later.

She fled out the main office door and down the hallway, literally running for the elevator.

Please be there. Please be there.

Ally didn't want to wait for one of the elevators to get to the top floor. She wanted out of this building and away from Travis. Now!

She punched the down button impatiently, over and over, as though it would open the elevator door faster. Her vision was blurred by her tears as she bolted into the elevator and pushed the button for the lobby.

"Ally! Goddammit! Wait!" There was a desperation in Travis's hoarse shout that she'd never heard before, but it didn't melt the ice that had formed around her heart.

Travis was a billionaire, a manipulative man who was used to getting everything his way. And he hadn't one iota of remorse for taking away a job she needed, so she could be at his beck and call if he needed her, whenever he needed her, and for whatever reason he needed her. *Bastard!* Did he think she was going to become his fuck buddy who he could call any time he wanted to take her out and play with her? Pathetically, she'd fallen under his thrall, and maybe he thought he could do just that now that she'd split with Rick. For the brief period of time when Travis had her body under his control, she'd thought she felt a connection, a deeper understanding between them. Oh, had she been so damn wrong.

He was sprinting for the elevator just as the doors were closing. For an instant, their eyes locked, and Ally could see despondency in his eyes as he caught a glimpse of her face. Or she thought she did. But it really didn't matter. She turned her head, unable to look at him, as the elevator doors slammed shut.

"Ally!" Travis's voice carried through the closed doors.

She pounded on the button for the lobby, willing the elevator to move. It jerked and went into motion, but it stopped on several floors on the way down, letting people in and out of the elevator on the way to the ground floor. Ally turned her face away, swiping at her cheeks to dry the tears on her face, hoping nobody would notice.

She stepped out of the elevator to the lobby as Travis came pounding out of the stairwell, his hair a mess, tendrils plastered to his forehead from taking so many flights of stairs in record time. "Ally. I need to talk to you."

She didn't want to talk to *him*. The last thing she needed right now was a lecture from *Mr. Harrison*. She flew out of the automatic doors and into the Florida heat, running as fast as she could in her stocking feet, juggling her clothing and shoes, digging her keys out of her purse as she went. She turned her head just as her feet hit the parking lot, trying to see if she was going to make it to her car before Travis caught up with her. He was almost close enough to touch, so she blindly bolted, seeing a brief moment of horror on Travis's face as his feet left the ground in an explosive vault toward her. The impact with his powerful body slammed into her, and she sailed through the air locked together with him briefly before landing on the pavement with a slow skid alone for a moment, Travis quickly moving and rolling her on top of him. She shook her head, confused, before she rested her head on his chest, the fall having scrambled her senses.

From beneath her, she vaguely heard Travis calling her name hoarsely, the sound rumbling against her ear.

Strangely, the only thought she could form in her mind was that today, for the first time since she'd known him, Travis was actually calling her "Ally."

"Are you sure you're okay?" Kade Harrison looked dubiously at his twin as he handed him a bag full of Duoderm, bandages, and ibuprofen. He dropped the overnight bag he had brought at Travis's request to Ally's house.

"We can stay with Ally," Asha suggested quietly, looking at Travis quizzically.

"I'm staying with her," Travis growled, not willing to relinquish Ally's care to anyone after watching her nearly get plowed down by a truck in the parking lot of Harrison. "This is my fault. I made her run in front of that truck. I should have explained everything to her immediately."

Kade shifted and folded his arms in front of him. "I'm not going to ask exactly how this happened because I doubt you'd tell me, but Ally's lucky that all she has is a bad case of road rash. I have a feeling you took most of the impact and you kept both of you from getting smashed by that truck. I'm asking if you're okay."

Travis wasn't about to tell his brother that his leg and back hurt like a son of a bitch. After what Kade had been through, Travis's aches and pains were minor, and the slight road rash on his face would heal. Ally had gotten it worse, her bare arms and back scraped by the unforgiving gravel and pavement. He hadn't quite been able to save her from the skid across the concrete from the impact of his body plowing into her. Since he'd been heavily covered from the neck down, all he had to bitch about was the soreness from the impact. "She could have died," Travis told his brother huskily.

Travis knew he'd never forget the moment he saw the truck come barreling into the parking lot, Ally running right into its path. He shuddered as he thought about what could have happened, what had almost happened. Although he'd managed to throw them both clear of the oncoming truck, Ally had still gotten hurt. Because of him.

"She didn't, Travis," Kade told his brother solemnly. "You were there."

I caused it. It was my fault.

Travis suddenly wanted to unload his guilty conscience, tell Kade everything, but he didn't. "I'm sticking around to help her. You two can go on home. It's not like we haven't both had road rash a time or two." That was putting it mildly. Since they were both addicted to moving at high rates of speed on anything with an engine, they'd both had their fair share of accidents in childhood and as adults.

Kade gave Travis a knowing grin. "I brought everything you'll need."

Travis had taken Ally to the hospital, and they'd cleaned the debris from her wounds. But he knew from experience they'd start to hurt like hell very shortly. Road rash usually hurt more later than right when it happened, the small nerve endings starting to protest some hours after the actual injury.

"Call us," Asha insisted. "I want to know how you're both doing." She walked up to Travis and kissed him on the cheek, avoiding the area that was scraped up.

Travis shifted uncomfortably, still not used to Asha's open affection. It wasn't that he didn't like it…exactly. He just wasn't used to it. The only woman who had ever shown him that kind of affection was Mia, and Tate's sister, Chloe.

Travis caught Kade's smirk and he scowled at him. Kade knew damn good and well that Asha unsettled him when she treated him like a brother. He was a cold bastard, an asshole, and he didn't handle open affection very well.

"Thanks," Travis grumbled to Asha awkwardly, giving Kade another dirty look.

"I'll handle the stuff at Harrison for a while. Just take care of Ally," Kade suggested, wrapping his arm around his pregnant wife. "And go easy on the hero stuff, would you? You took ten years off my life today when I heard you were at the hospital."

Travis shot his brother a grim look. "Now you know how I felt," he admitted, remembering the day of Kade's accident.

"I'm supposed to be the wild twin," Kade told him with a chuckle as he led Asha to the door. "Seriously, call me if you need anything. Harrison will survive without you for a while."

"It will have to," Travis replied, not even giving business a thought at the moment. His main concern was Ally.

Travis locked the door behind them, grabbing his bag and the medical supplies as he returned to the living room.

"Why are you still here?" Ally's hollow voice came from the bottom of the stairs.

"You're hurt. I'm not leaving. Once those road burns start to hurt, you might need help." He shot her an obstinate look, a warning that he wasn't going anywhere.

"No offense, but you look worse than I do," she answered matter-of-factly, coming the rest of the way into the living room, dressed in a thick, green robe that covered her from neck to ankles.

She'd showered, her damp hair just starting to curl on the ends. "It's just my face, and it's superficial," he said, dismissing her comment.

Travis watched her as she sat down with a wince, curling her legs under her in a recliner. He dropped his overnight bag and took the sack Kade had brought him out to the kitchen, rifling through it for the ibuprofen. After shaking a few into his palm, he grabbed a can of soda from the refrigerator and brought them back to Ally. "Take these," he demanded, handing her the can and dropping the medicine into her open hand.

"I'm just scraped up, Travis. You can go now," she told him adamantly after she'd swallowed the pills. "I'm grateful for what you did today. The truck driver said he probably would have hit me if you hadn't prevented it. So thank you for saving me from that. But I'd prefer it if you left."

Travis shed the ruined jacket of his suit and rolled up the sleeves of his shirt, taking a seat across from Ally on the couch. "I didn't mean to hurt you, Ally. And I'm not letting you quit."

Ally snorted weakly. "What are you going to do, Mr. Harrison? Handcuff me to my desk?"

Travis's cock twitched over that remark, but he ignored it. "No."

"Since you already lost me a position I needed, you'd have to for me to ever set foot in that office again." Ally sighed deeply. "I can't work for you anymore because—"

"I raised your salary effective immediately," Travis confessed. "I knew you wouldn't leave the bar, and I couldn't watch you work yourself into the ground. I asked Sullivan what your average salary with tips was at Sully's, and I raised your annual salary by a little more than that amount. You don't need to work there anymore. I thought that was what you wanted. I thought you wanted to have some time to pursue your other dreams. It was actually supposed to be a birthday surprise. When I got back to the office late, I was afraid I'd missed you. I wanted to take you out for dinner for your birthday and give you something you really wanted. When I saw you in that *fuck-me* lingerie, I forgot about everything else." Not one single other thing in the world had mattered when he'd seen Ally in his office looking like an erotic fantasy. He'd needed to touch her, make her as crazy with need as he had been at that moment. There was only so much a guy could take, and he'd reached his limit when he saw her.

Ally gaped at him for a moment before she replied hesitantly. "So it wasn't really for your convenience, was it?"

"Yes and no. It's convenient knowing you're safer and happier, but that isn't why I did it. I do suppose there was some selfish motivation involved." Hell, he couldn't let her think that he was that altruistic, because he wasn't. "But it wasn't really about me wanting you available to me all the time. Ally, when have I ever demanded you be available after hours? I might be an asshole, but I usually do it during work hours."

"Then why did you say that?" Her green eyes flashed a look of confusion.

"Because I'm an asshole?" he asked, trying to lighten the conversation.

Ally nodded. "Agreed." She looked at him, her eyes searching his face. "Are you doing all this because we're attracted to each other?"

Did she mean was he doing it because he wanted to fuck her more than he wanted to breathe? Maybe...or maybe not...he wasn't quite sure. All he knew was that she'd been screwed over by her ex, and he wanted to make her life easier. "You deserve the raise. You've become more of an assistant than a secretary over the years, taking on more and more responsibility."

She looked at him doubtfully. "You already pay me at the high end of the scale for my position."

"For a secretarial position. I promoted you to executive assistant," he told her calmly. "Now you're on the high end of that scale." Okay…that was a little bit of a stretch. She was still salaried higher than the top of the scale, but dammit, it was his company and Ally did the work of both an assistant and a secretary. He'd never needed anyone else. She was worth that and more.

She cocked her brow at him. "It's still a secretarial position, Travis. It's just a more important sounding title. Why are you really doing this?"

"I thought I already explained that," he grumbled irritably. Christ! Couldn't the woman just take the damn raise and promotion without arguing about it? "You've had to put up with me for four years. Before that, I couldn't keep an assistant or a secretary." That was totally true. He was an anal perfectionist, and nobody had performed like Ally had as an assistant or a secretary. She anticipated his needs before he even realized what he needed, on a professional level anyway.

"And you couldn't have discussed all this with me first?" she questioned quietly.

"No. Then it wouldn't have been a surprise." And he hadn't planned on letting her refuse.

"You just can't go around arranging people's lives, Travis. I appreciate what you were trying to do, but I'm a grown woman, and I make my own decisions."

"Since when?" he challenged. "Every decision you've made over the last several years has been for your idiot ex, and he certainly never cared whether it was something you wanted or not. It was all for him. What the hell does it matter if I'm giving you something that *you* actually want?" Travis wasn't used to being questioned when he actually did something nice, which he almost never did, and he managed people's lives all the time, usually because they didn't do it very well themselves.

She was silent for a moment, giving him a quizzical stare. "And what exactly are my new duties?"

Hell, Travis hadn't really thought about that. She already did the work of two employees. "We'll make it up as we go along."

"I'm not sleeping with you," Ally warned him with a frown.

Travis folded his arms in front of him unhappily and stared back at her. "You will. But when it happens, it won't be because it's part of your job description. You'll do it freely because you want to."

Ally took a swig of her soda before replying, "Don't count on it."

"And you'll bring me my coffee every morning as part of your new duties," he informed her.

She shook her head. "Absolutely not."

He'd already known she'd say that, but he didn't care. As long as she was safe and he could persuade her to come back to work for him, he could live with that.

Chapter 7

When Ally awoke the next day, it was almost noon. How long had it been since she'd slept this late? She stretched, grimacing as her body protested the sudden movement. As usual, Travis was right: the scraped areas on her skin hurt more now than they had the day before.

Was he still here?

She got carefully out of bed, snatching up her robe to put it on over her skimpy nightshirt. Travis had sent her off to bed, telling her he'd be there if she needed anything. Had he really stayed just to make sure she was going to be okay? Really, the infuriating man was confounding her. One moment he was his same asshole self, and then a moment later he was making her shake her head in confusion. It pissed her off that he'd meddled in her life. Yet, what he had done was also one of the nicest things anyone had ever done for her, even if it was highhanded and arrogant. Strangely enough, she believed him when he said he hadn't done it for himself. But the unselfish actions just weren't consistent with the Travis she knew. Certainly, she'd see him do some amazing things for his family, things they probably weren't even aware he'd done for them. However, she was hardly family, simply a valuable employee.

Curious, she wandered downstairs, passing all the bathroom and bedroom doors as she went, every room open and empty. Travis's bag was sitting on the bed in the master bedroom, the same room that she refused to use because Rick had banged his girlfriend on that bed. The proof of Travis's presence in that room gave her a sort of deranged sense of satisfaction, the thought of him tussled and sleeping in that bed somehow exorcising a few of the ghostly images of the past.

Ally stopped abruptly as she entered the kitchen, eyeing the piles of papers on her kitchen table, Travis sitting in one of the chairs, moving papers from one pile to the next. He grumbled, and then dumped a sheet of paper on one of the piles, moving to the next with the intense concentration she saw on his face every day at work.

"What are you doing?" she asked, perplexed, noticing her box where she filed all her papers sitting beside his elbow.

Travis looked up at her, his dark eyes roving over her body and coming to rest on her face. "Contemplating how much I'd like to put your ex in the hospital for an extended stay. He'd be there right now if I didn't think it would just cause more problems for you."

Ally opened her mouth and closed it again, taking in the frustrated look on Travis's face. For once, he didn't look immaculate. He looked dangerously disheveled, his hair mussed as though he'd been running his hand through it over and over again. "Are those my personal papers?"

Travis shrugged. "How personal are bills?"

"Why are you going through my bills? How dare you?" Her outrage and curiosity were warring with each other as she asked.

"You said you needed to clean up the mess your ex made of your life so you can move on. So I'm cleaning it up." Travis stated the fact with utter calm, giving her a questioning look like he didn't understand why she'd protest. "You made it quite easy to find everything, by the way. You're very organized. Everything was alphabetized. Although I'm not quite sure 'asshole ex' is quite the way you're supposed to label and file certain bills."

Ally took a deep breath and let it out, not knowing whether to laugh or strangle Travis. "I said I need to figure everything out. I can't believe you're going through my bills."

"I'm finished, actually," Travis stated calmly, picking up the piles and replacing them into her filing box. "And if you were engaged, why is it that the asshole never bought you a ring? Or did you just not wear it?"

"He didn't. He said we couldn't afford it."

"He bought one. He charged it." Travis gave her a concerned glance. "After you split up. Why the hell didn't you take him off your accounts?"

"He bought it for her," Ally said flatly, nausea starting to rise from her stomach to her throat, horrified once again because she'd been so stupid. "I only looked at the balances. I couldn't bring myself to see *what* he bought. He never bought me a single piece of jewelry the whole time we were together. Yet he used *my* cards and credit to charge thousands on things for *her*?" Ally paused for a second to get her emotions under control. "I was naïve. I guess it never occurred to me that a man I spent five years with would ever run up debt in my name after he'd already betrayed me."

"Stupid fucking bastard," Travis growled, closing the top on the box with a gigantic *slam*.

Ally felt her eyes well up with tears, an overwhelming sense of worthlessness leaving her stunned. "I wasn't important enough. No matter what I did, it wasn't enough."

"Don't cry," Travis told her ominously. "He isn't worth it. It's over. Everything is paid and you can move on again, Ally. He was a leach, a bloodsucker who doesn't care about anyone except himself. It had nothing to do with you. Most men would kill to have a woman like you. It's him, not you."

Travis's voice was so matter-of-fact, so sincere that it made Ally want to cry even more. "I have to pay you back. I'm not your family, Travis. You can't just move in and take over my life." She wanted to tell him off, be angry that he'd butted into her business. But really, what he was doing was one of the sweetest things anyone had ever done for her, so she was having a hard time getting pissed off at him. Travis was bullheaded, and he was used to managing everything. But when had a man actually listened or cared about what she wanted, offering—or actually demanding—that she let him help make her dreams come true?

"I thought you wanted everything in the past." Travis sounded confused. "And no, I'm not family, which is really a pretty disgusting thought when you take into consideration how desperately I want to fuck you. That would be awkward."

Ally sighed. She had no doubt that Travis did want to screw her, but she had no idea why. "Is that why you're doing this?" Men just didn't run around paying their employees' bills and organizing their lives for them to make things better for no reason.

"No," Travis answered huskily. "I guess I just wanted to make you smile at me."

That answered floored her. She searched Travis's face, the scrapes he'd gotten from saving her life the day before still evident. With his hair mussed, his face littered with red marks, his clothes consisting of casual black jeans and a dark pullover, he looked almost...vulnerable.

Her lips trembled for a moment as she caught her breath, astounded. And then, she just couldn't help herself; she smiled like a madwoman. Yes, she was pissed that he'd pawed through her personal files, but his desire to please her was there on his face, and that made her heart sing. Travis Harrison, billionaire extraordinaire, had actually taken the morning to help her, wanting nothing more than to see her happy. "Is this good enough?" she asked him, still smiling broadly as she made her way over to the coffee pot. "And we *are* going to have to talk about how I'll pay you back and about how wrong it is to rifle through personal papers."

Travis squirmed. "That smile was good enough for an all-day boner."

Ally giggled as she poured herself a cup of coffee. She couldn't help it. "But you wanted it," she reminded him.

"I still do. But it will be damn uncomfortable. I guess I'll just have to spend another night in your bed jacking off to fantasies about fucking you," he said bluntly. "But I can guarantee just my fantasies about you were better than his sex with his bimbo could ever be."

Ally nearly choked on her coffee. Her body heated at thoughts of Travis's ripped, naked body, and him stroking himself in her bed while he thought about doing wicked things to her. "You didn't," she denied.

"Oh, I did," Travis replied evilly. "And it was immensely satisfying to know that I was probably getting more pleasure in that bed with my fantasies about you than he ever did with his girlfriend."

Okay...maybe he actually did. And that made Ally even hotter. If the ghosts of her ex screwing another woman in that room hadn't already been exorcised, they certainly were now. Changing the subject, she sat down next to him at the table. "Can we talk about my new job title and repayment terms?" She certainly couldn't spend one more moment thinking about Travis touching himself.

"No," he answered simply, picking up his own coffee and taking a slug. "Consider it a bonus. Although I wouldn't argue if you let me be the first person to read the second book in your fantasy series. You left me hanging."

"You actually read the first one?" she asked, amazed. He had to have read the manuscript almost immediately to have already finished it.

"I said I wanted to read it. It's good, Ally. Really good. You need to finish it. Does the young hero eventually get his princess?"

He'd said he wanted to read her book, but people said those things all the time. They didn't necessarily mean it. Obviously, he had read the story if he knew about the hero and the princess. "My hero is a little young for that right now." She took a small sip of her coffee. "You don't strike me as the type of guy to read young adult fantasy."

"I grew up reading fantasy," Travis answered thoughtfully. "*The Chronicles of Narnia* series was one of my favorites. I remember looking in every closet we had, trying to find a secret door so I could take Kade and Mia away somewhere else after reading the first book."

Ally's heart began to bleed for him, thinking about a young Travis trying to escape his horrible childhood. "I loved that series." It had been one of her favorites too, liking it for much the same reasons as Travis: to escape her miserable childhood.

"You need to write, Ally. Finish the books. You're talented. I have no idea why the book was rejected, but books like yours brighten the lives of a lot of young people. They can escape into a dream when everything else in their life isn't so great." Travis eyed her with a pensive expression before digging into his pocket and pulling out a velvet box. "I missed your birthday, but this made me think of you. I meant to give it to you yesterday."

Ally stared at the fancy box Travis was holding for a moment before reaching out a trembling hand to take it. She wasn't used to getting gifts, and especially not from men. "Why?" she asked nervously.

"It's a reminder to follow your dreams. And a belated birthday present. It's nothing really," Travis told her tensely, as though he felt a little awkward.

Ally popped the lid, gasping as she saw the contents. There, nestled in a bed of red velvet, was the most exquisite necklace she'd ever seen. But it wasn't the diamonds or the sapphires that immediately caught her eye, but the design. It was a small unicorn, the entire body sparkling with white diamonds, the horn and eyes made of small blue sapphires. "My unicorn," she said breathlessly, taking in what was almost an exact tiny replica of the unicorn from her books.

"It doesn't talk like yours does, but I'm hoping that you'll remember to write every time you wear it," Travis told her huskily.

Tears rolled down Ally's cheeks as she fingered the delicate, beautiful beast on the gold chain. "I don't know what to say." And she didn't. No one had ever given her such a thoughtful gift. "The first piece of jewelry I've ever gotten as a gift," she mumbled tearfully. "It's beautiful." She also knew it was expensive. "Travis, it's too expensive of a gift for me to accept."

"Bullshit. I said it was nothing," he rumbled. "I'm not taking it back unless you don't like it. Then I'll get you something else."

"I love it," she cried anxiously. "But I don't get gifts like this. It's too much. But it's incredible."

"It's nothing compared to what I want to give you, Ally. And I still want to be the first to read the next book," he demanded.

Ally looked up from the sparkling unicorn to look into his eyes, eyes that were turbulent and uncomfortable, as though he wasn't quite sure how to express himself. "You believe in my writing that much?"

"Not just your writing. I believe in you," he admitted, his tone sincere.

Her heart ready to pound out of her chest, Ally rose and went to Travis, putting her arms around him gently and kissing him lightly on the cheek. "Thank you," she whispered, unable to express how much his faith meant to her. She wanted to tell him, wanted to let him know how much his support meant to her after what she'd gone through with her ex, but the lump in her throat wouldn't let her say anything else. So she just hugged him, tears still rolling down her cheeks. "I love this, and I'm keeping it. It will always remind me that one person actually liked my book," she told him lightheartedly, knowing emotion wasn't something Travis dealt with easily. "And we *will* talk about repayment for the bills." She let him go reluctantly and sat back in her chair.

"No, we won't," Travis answered in a graveled voice. "And that hug was good for an all-week boner."

She laughed, amused by the disgruntled look on his face. She highly doubted Travis got excited over a simple hug, but he was good for her battered ego. Travis Harrison could get any woman he wanted, any time he wanted one. But she let the compliments wash over her, let the fact that he found her attractive warm her soul. "I can't believe you didn't go into the office today. Are we working tomorrow?" she asked, knowing Travis never missed a day of work.

"Hell, no. And I'll need to bandage those wounds again later. You aren't going to feel like working for a while. You're starting vacation early." Travis shot her an obstinate look.

Ally rolled her eyes. "I'm fine. You don't need to take care of me."

"I'm going to," he replied irritably. "So get used to it."

Ally crossed her arms in front of her, secretly loving his protectiveness, but confused by it at the same time. "Why? I'm just an employee. It's not like I'm Mia or Kade. I can understand that you meddle in their life. But why me?"

"I don't meddle in their lives," Travis answered grumpily.

"Oh, so you didn't really make Mia disappear for two years so her ex couldn't harm her, and didn't tell a single soul except your security? And you just happened to be in Colorado when that same ex had a fatal car accident?" Did Travis think she was completely blind and deaf? She was his assistant. She saw and heard everything that happened in his office for the most part.

"What the hell do you know about that?" Travis shot her a laser-sharp glance.

"I know that Mia called looking for you the day before she disappeared and she sounded upset. Then she disappeared the next day. Every single day after that, you had an early morning security meeting, something you'd never done before. You've never given a crap about your own security. And I know you distanced yourself from Kade and Max. Most of all, I know you didn't grieve like I know you would if you thought something had really happened to your sister."

"All that time, you knew?" Travis answered incredulously. "And you never told a soul."

"Why would I? I realized you were somehow trying to protect her," Ally asked, baffled. "Why would I jeopardize her safety? I'm your assistant. I'd never betray you."

"How could you know for sure I was protecting her? What if I'd done something to her to try to get rid of her? I could have wanted her share of the stocks and the business."

Ally snorted. Obviously Travis had never seen himself when he looked at Mia, his love for her showing in the depth of his eyes. Maybe he didn't express himself well, but his love for his sister was evident. "Not possible," Ally answered adamantly. "I didn't understand everything that was going on, but I know how much you care about Mia, and that was all I needed to know."

"He assaulted her, beat her, and blackmailed her," Travis admitted hoarsely. "When I finally caught up with him, he bolted. I followed. He conveniently ran his car off a cliff. But I made it happen. I killed him. And I've never had one pang of remorse. I was just glad the bastard was dead so he couldn't kill my sister."

"I'm glad, too," Ally affirmed.

"It doesn't scare you that I'm a killer?" Travis asked, his gaze dark and unfathomable.

"No. You did what you needed to do to protect Mia. I'm just sorry you had to bear that burden alone."

"I had to. I couldn't risk Max and Kade giving away her location," Travis said, his voice tinged with remorse.

Ally wondered if Kade and Max really knew the price Travis had paid to *not* tell them, taking on the burden of knowledge completely alone. "You love your siblings, Travis. I've always known that. I don't think you ever missed one of Kade's football games. Did he even know you were always there?" Ally had always been the one to make the arrangements for Travis's jet to fly him to wherever Kade was playing, and fly him back the same day.

Travis shrugged. "I didn't want to make him nervous. I just wanted to be there."

I just wanted to be there. Ally suddenly realized that his statement really summed up just who Travis was: a man who wanted to support his siblings and didn't care whether he ever got credit for being an incredible brother to them. More than likely, neither Mia nor Kade ever realized just how often Travis had been there for them without them ever really knowing about it. Did Mia know how much heat Travis had taken in order to keep her hidden and safe, how much he'd had to isolate himself from his own brother and brother-in-law? Did she know how much Max and Kade had resented him for what he did? Did Kade realize that Travis had made every one of his games, and how devastated Travis had been about Kade's accident? He'd spent almost every waking moment at the hospital after his brother's accident. "You're an incredible brother, Travis Harrison," Ally told him quietly. "I would have given anything to have someone like you."

"Still don't want to be your brother," Travis answered belligerently. "I want to fuck you too much." He got up and went to the kitchen counter, shaking her out some ibuprofen and handing it to her. "Take these. We'll need to change those bandages."

Ally took the pills from his hand and swallowed them with a sip of coffee. "They're really just scratches, Travis."

He scowled at her as he answered, "You don't need to get them infected." He winced as he sat back down.

"You're hurting," Ally commented suspiciously. "Did you injure yourself? I thought you were covered."

"Just bruises from hitting the concrete," Travis answered, blowing off her concern. "Not a big deal."

"You're in pain. Let me see," she told him in a no-nonsense voice.

Travis obediently turned in his chair and lifted his shirt. Ally gasped as she saw a contusion the size of her hand on his lower back. She reached her hand out and touched it lightly with a fingertip. "Oh my God, Travis. I'm so sorry."

"I landed on a parking block when I hit the ground. It will heal," he replied gruffly.

"You might need x-rays. What if you broke something?"

"I didn't. I've had enough injuries to know."

"Are there more? Where do they stop?" Ally was appalled and sick over the fact that she hadn't known that Travis had been injured.

Travis turned his head slowly and shot her the wickedest grin she'd ever seen. "Sweetheart, to show you all of them I'd have to drop my pants. But I'd be more than happy to show you if you'll touch them all."

Ally gulped, torn between wanting to see the bruises and knowing she really shouldn't watch her billionaire boss drop his pants. "Are they bad?" she croaked.

"The one on my back is probably the worst. It's where I hit the parking block. But I'll be happy to show you." He started to get up.

"No, no," she said hastily. "I'll take your word for it. But if the pain gets bad, we're taking you for x-rays. I can't believe you're worried about a few little scrapes on me when you're all bruised up. Are you hurting anywhere else?"

Travis slowly sat back down. "My cock is hurting. Do you want to touch it?" he asked coarsely, but the look in his eyes was teasing and devilish.

Ally's whole face turned red, Travis's blunt words leaving her speechless for a moment. "You have a dirty mind," she chastised him lightly. "And I'm truly worried about you hurting."

"I am hurting. And that's the worse ache I have," Travis told her bluntly as he eyed her hungrily.

His predatory gaze made her even redder. Hell, she hadn't blushed like this since she was in high school. Travis had shown her another side of himself, and she liked it, liked *him* right now. But his feral gaze unnerved her in ways that had her almost panting to touch him. "You're bruised up and you can still think about *that*?"

"Alison, I'd have to be dead to not want you to touch me," Travis answered gravely.

Ally shivered, her core flooding with heat, her nipples going as hard as pebbles from the intensity of his stare. Problem was, she felt exactly the same way. She looked away from him, unable to bear the heat in his eyes. One second longer, and she'd be begging him to let her touch him. "No touching," she told him much more adamantly than she felt right at that moment. "You need to heal." Ally got up and put her empty mug in the sink, cradling her precious gift from Travis in her hand.

"I was afraid you'd say that," Travis answered unhappily, rising to put his own cup in the sink.

"Thank you for this," Ally whispered, gesturing toward the necklace. "It's the most incredible gift I've ever received. It means a lot to me." It wasn't the monetary value, but the significance of the actual symbol, a sign of Travis's belief in her writing.

Ally wandered toward the entry to the kitchen, heading off to the shower.

"Ally?" Travis's voice sounded hesitantly from where she'd left him by the sink.

"Yeah?" She turned her head.

"Thanks for not betraying me," he said hoarsely.

"You don't need to thank me for that, Travis. You've always had my loyalty." And he had. He might infuriate her, but there was never a time she had doubted Travis's integrity or his love for his family.

He nodded abruptly and turned away, leaving Ally wondering what had just happened between them. Their relationship had shifted, leaving her wondering if it were actually possible for her and Travis to become...friends.

Travis melted her with just one glance, set her on fire with his sultry voice and his naughty comments. But she had to ignore both, wait until he found another love interest. Being anything else to Travis except his employee and friend was dangerous. She'd already been devastated when she'd thought he'd betrayed her trust by getting her fired from Sully's, almost running in front of a moving truck because she was so distraught. Ally could only imagine how bad things would be if she actually allowed herself to become more intimate than she'd already been with him. Travis left her raw and vulnerable, elated but terrified. Getting too close to him would be a mistake, and there would be no turning back once she allowed him in. His intensity would overwhelm her, and she'd be left to pick up the pieces of the devastation after the affair was over.

"Don't fall for him, Ally. Keep him at a distance," she told herself forcefully as she went up the stairs.

Her sense of self-preservation back in place, she went to take a shower, hoping she could manage to keep her resolve.

Chapter 8

Travis stayed the entire weekend, never once leaving Ally's house except to get something he was absolutely certain she needed. He'd left reluctantly on Monday morning, after Ally had insisted she would be fine without him. That weekend had been a revelation for her, showing her more and more just what an incredible person Travis could be in a different atmosphere away from the office. They'd watched movies for hours, played several games of chess, a game that Ally had always thought she'd excelled at...until she'd played a master like Travis. He'd trounced her every single time. And they'd talked. Sometimes they'd discussed inconsequential things, but he'd opened up a little about what his childhood had been like, being raised with a volatile and insane father. And she'd shared some of her own memories of being raised by an alcoholic and how isolated and out of control she'd felt when she was younger. By the time he'd left on Monday...she actually missed him almost as soon as he'd walked out the door. The house felt strangely quiet, and she hated having her coffee alone in the morning, not having anyone to talk to when she had something to say.

Tuesday and Wednesday, Ally was too busy receiving deliveries to really think about her loneliness. The doorbell rang almost nonstop, bringing so many deliveries that her living room was stacked with boxes, most of them containing items for a brand new wardrobe that Travis had provided. Of course, she'd called him to protest, and Travis told her to refer to her new employment contract, which apparently had a clause about him providing work attire.

Ally looked around the living room and rolled her eyes. *Work attire?* The room contained more clothing than an actual high-end boutique, everything from lingerie to ball gowns. And every single item fit perfectly, even the shoes and boots. How the hell had he known exactly what size to buy?

"Because he's Travis Harrison and he doesn't do anything without paying attention to every detail," she whispered to herself, sitting down on the small space of her couch that was still available. "I can't take all this stuff. There isn't a thing in this lot that isn't designer-made and horribly expensive."

Ally started lifting boxes, finally locating her cell phone under some sinful lingerie.

I'm sending this stuff back. You only promised to get me a dress for Colorado. That's more than enough.

She sent the text, determined to decide on one item for the ball in Colorado that she had to attend with Travis.

He responded moments later:

Can't. It was all on sale and non-returnable. Don't you like it?

Ally sighed, laughing out loud at the reference to a sale. Not very creative or believable coming from Travis. She texted him back.

It's too much. One dress is good enough.

She was startled when her phone rang, already knowing it was Travis.

"Beautiful women should have beautiful clothes," Travis said huskily in her ear before she could even say anything. "I do get to provide your clothing for you. Read your contract."

"Is there anything else in this contract that I signed but didn't read that I should know about?" she asked, frustrated, wishing she'd looked just a little bit closer at the contract Travis had asked her to sign over the weekend. But she'd assumed it was just the ordinary stuff, much like the employment contracts she'd signed for Harrison previously. Travis knew damn well that when he said things like that he threw her off-balance. She wasn't used to being called beautiful or even remotely attractive.

"Didn't you see the part about me being able to fuck you any way I want to as many times a day as we both want it?" he asked lazily, as though he were having a business conversation.

Ally's entire body flooded with heat. Tired of letting Travis always get the upper hand with his sexual banter, she answered him in a *fuck-me* voice that she wasn't even aware she was capable of producing. "No. I only noticed the clause that says I can drop to my knees, pull out your cock, and wrap my lips around it any time I want, sucking you until you come."

She heard a hiss come from Travis's end of the line, and she smiled a naughty little grin. *Bang! Take that Mr. Dirty Talker!*

The line was absolutely silent for a moment before Travis responded in a pained voice, "I'll make you pay for that, Alison."

"You can dish it out, but you can't take it?" she asked innocently.

"I'll be taking it," Travis answered ominously. "Dinner tonight," he demanded. "I'll pick you up around seven."

"Do I have a choice?" she asked in an exasperated voice.

"Yes. You can wear the red lingerie or the black. I pictured fucking you in both of them," he answered hoarsely.

The line went dead, Travis obviously not willing to give her a chance to argue. She'd actually gotten to him, shaken him up a bit with her own slam back at him.

Maybe she should be upset that she hadn't really talked him into taking some of the clothes back, or irritated because he'd just assumed she'd go out to dinner with him. But the only emotion she felt at the moment was a giddiness that bubbled up inside her at the thought of seeing Travis again.

She laughed and started going through the boxes for something to wear that evening.

Travis leaned back in his office chair and closed his eyes, trying not to look at the desk and picture Ally sprawled out on top of it, abandoned and desperate. He tried not to hear her husky moans of pleasure as she splintered apart as she came for him.

Fuck! He hated that damn desk. It was like torture working in his office every day, trying not to think about what had happened on top of that very desk. Sometimes he even swore he caught her scent every now and then, a ghostly aroma of what she had smelled like in her arousal.

Her words about sucking him off went through his mind over and over again, making his cock rock-hard, and his fists clench on top of the desk. "I need a new fucking desk," he said harshly, thinking in reality what he needed was an exorcism. Ally haunted him almost every minute of every day. And it had gotten even worse since he'd spent the weekend with her, realizing how much he adored just about everything about her. Hearing about her childhood and her vulnerabilities just made him even more protective, more determined to make her life everything she deserved.

"You paid a fortune for that desk. Why would you want to get rid of it?" Kade's voice sounded from just inside Travis's office door.

Opening his eyes, Travis gave his twin a disgusted look. "I don't."

"I'll take it if you want to replace it," Kade said casually, closing the door and moving to drop into the chair in front of Travis's desk.

Oh, hell no. No way was Kade going to be using the desk that Travis had used when he'd made Ally come for the first time. "No," he answered angrily.

"Okay. Fine." Kade held up a hand in defeat. "I thought I heard you say you wanted a new desk. I was just offering to take it off your hands. I wanted to see how Ally was doing. Have you heard from her?"

"Yeah. She's doing okay," Travis told his brother in a milder tone. "I just wish she was back. The office doesn't run the same without her here."

"You miss fighting with her," Kade said teasingly.

"I miss everything about her," Travis admitted. "She's...efficient."

"Her ex really did a number on her. Asha told me about it," Kade replied, his voice tinged with anger.

"I'd like to kill him, but I think it would upset Ally," Travis said morosely.

"You have it pretty bad for her, don't you?" Kade asked quietly. "Don't deny it, Trav. I've known for a while now."

"How did you know?" Travis eyed his brother warily.

"I have it bad myself. I can see the signs. I think you've always fought with Ally to keep her at a distance. How long?"

Travis sighed, not wanted to admit it, but needing to talk to Kade. "Since the fucking day I hired her. There were more experienced applicants, people who had better qualifications. But I must be a damn masochist, because I hired her anyway. I couldn't stand the thought of not seeing her again."

"Does she know?" Kade asked quietly.

"She should. I tell her every damn day that I want to fuck her," Travis grumbled.

Kade coughed hard several times before gasping. "Very romantic and smooth, Trav. Is that all you want from her?"

Was it? Travis didn't exactly know. "I don't do romance, and all I know is that the woman drives me crazy."

"She was hurt pretty badly, Travis. Ally may act tough, but she's fragile right now. Her self-esteem was battered. If all you want is a fuck, get it somewhere else."

Travis slammed his fist down on the wooden desk, making everything on the surface rattle. "Don't you think I've tried? I don't want anyone else. I can't do another woman. I just want her. I want to kill any man who looks at her, anyone who hurts her in any way. I want to give her anything and everything she wants. I want her to be happy, dammit."

Kade grinned at Travis. "Why didn't you try to take her away from her asshole ex before?"

"Because I didn't know he was a bastard. I thought she was happy. I'm an asshole, Kade. Everybody knows that. I thought she was better off with a nice guy."

"And now that she's single?" Kade prompted.

"She's mine," Travis growled. "I'm not giving her a chance to hook up with another loser. If she wants an asshole, she can just take me."

Kade chuckled before he answered more seriously, "It's your turn, Travis. You've spent your whole life taking care of the business, the employees, Mia, and me. It's time for you to figure out what you need."

"I need her," Travis replied desperately. "Christ. I don't know how you do it. How do you need a woman so much and survive?"

Kade smirked. "You don't. So you make damn sure you get her."

"She's stubborn," Travis grumbled. "She doesn't even want to take the new clothes I bought for her. It's in her damn contract. I provide her a new wardrobe."

Kade grimaced. "Women are funny that way. Asha did the same thing."

"And what did you do?"

"I ignored her protests. She got over it eventually and took them from Maddie as a gift from her sister."

"Ally complains pretty loud," Travis answered unhappily, knowing she'd make it difficult for him not to hear her. But he'd still try to ignore it. He wanted her to keep the clothes. Christ! It wasn't like he couldn't afford it.

"I know," Kade said happily. "It's one of the reasons I think she's perfect for you." He hesitated before asking, "What would you have done if Ally hadn't found out her ex was a dick? What if she had actually gotten married?"

"I don't know," Travis answered honestly. "I tried not to think about it, tried to tell myself it didn't matter. But if it came down to that day, that moment, I'm not so sure I wouldn't have done just about anything to keep it from happening. The only thing that had ever stopped me was the possibility of ruining her happiness. Shit! I have no idea how I never noticed how tired she was, or how miserable things were for her. I didn't know she had to work in a damn bar to make ends meet. I thought she had the perfect life, the perfect fiancé who was getting ready to start a prosperous career. I wanted her, but I didn't think I was the best thing for her." He was a murderer and an unfeeling bastard. He'd wanted Ally to have someone better than that.

"And now?" Kade asked solemnly.

"Now I'm taking her. After understanding the bullshit she put up with for years, even being with me would be better than that. I'd treat her good, Kade. I'd give her whatever she wanted."

"Nobody knew what Ally was going through. She hid it very well. It isn't your fault. I don't think any of us could see beneath her tough exterior," Kade told his brother thoughtfully. "I think she just needs a man who cares about her. From what Asha tells me, Ally's self-esteem got hammered pretty badly. This asshole has obviously been knocking her down mentally for years."

"He killed her dreams," Travis said harshly. "Not only did he betray her and leave her stuck with his bills, but he didn't support her writing either."

"Ally writes?" Kade asked, surprised.

"Yeah. Incredible stories. She's talented, and I'm not just saying that because I have a hard-on for her. She has a gift, and he never encouraged it. He made her give it up, manipulated her into thinking everything was her fault or her responsibility. All that the bastard wanted was a meal ticket to get him through school. I'm pretty sure he actually had no intention of going through with the wedding at all. He just played on all of Ally's weaknesses to get her to support him." Travis clenched his fists on top of the desk, wishing he had his hands around Ally's ex's neck. "She's so damn smart and beautiful. I don't know how he managed to convince her otherwise. But he did. Bastard!"

"Sometimes we don't always see ourselves the way others do, Trav. If someone beats you down long enough, you start to believe it," Kade replied sadly. "Ally obviously doesn't see her own worth anymore except for her work. She may be confident in her job, but not in her value as a person. Look at what happened with Asha."

Travis knew what Kade was saying was true, knew what it was like to be beaten down until you couldn't see reality. He, Kade, and Mia had experienced that during their childhood and adolescence. Luckily, they'd all had one another. Travis had a hard time comparing Ally to Asha, their personalities on the surface so different. Asha was quieter, shyer. "Asha's getting better."

Kade nodded. "She is. But you and I both know that it takes time to undo years of conditioning. Asha and Ally have very different personalities, but I think the reason they became friends is because they understand each other in the ways that really matter."

"How can I fix her?" Travis asked huskily.

Kade laughed. "She's not a car, Travis. She's a woman. They're much more complicated."

"No shit. And you aren't much help." Travis glared at his twin.

"I think you'll figure it out. If you really care about her, that's all that really matters. It's a hell of a lot more than she's had in the past." Kade rose and strolled to the door. He turned around as he opened the door, looking first at Travis and then at his desk, and then smirked. "I think I figured out why you have a love/hate relationship with that desk."

Travis watched as his brother left the office, letting the door close quietly behind him, still trying to figure out exactly what Kade meant by that comment. Certainly, Kade couldn't know...

Shaking his head, Travis glanced at the clock, convinced that Kade could never guess why he was really having a "desk frustration" problem. It was three o'clock. Damn! Most days he didn't give a shit what time it was for any reason other than appointments. Now, he willed the damn clock to move faster.

Irritated, he pulled his cell phone out of his pocket and sent a text to Ally.

Six o'clock instead of seven.

There. That was one less hour he'd have to wait. At least he'd get to see her sooner. If Ally wasn't ready or she didn't get his message, then he'd just wait...or think of something else to fill the time...

He put his phone back in his pocket and turned back to his computer, wondering if he'd completely lost his mind, and thinking he was the most desperate, pathetic guy on the face of the earth. What the hell difference did an hour make?

His phone pinged that he had a text, and he dug it out again eagerly. It was from Ally, and there were no words, just a picture. He touched the image and it came up full screen, a photo of the delicate red lingerie with barely there red panties and a red garter belt.

Travis almost dropped the damn phone.

He groaned quietly and decided that an hour was going to make a hell of a lot of difference.

Chapter 9

Ally studied herself in the full-length mirror in her bedroom. It was only five thirty, but she was as ready as she was going to be. The red dress was simple, the neckline plunging a little more than she usually liked, and it clung to her hips in ways she wasn't exactly certain were good for her figure. But she thought she looked passable. She'd taken time with her hair and makeup, leaving her blonde locks down to caress her back and shoulders. The hem of the dress came almost to her knees, and the three-quarter length sleeves hid her healing road rash. The three-inch stilettos made walking a little precarious, but if she stepped carefully she'd be okay.

Ally wished, not for the first time, that she was thin and pretty. She sighed as she turned away from the mirror, chastising herself for caring. She was just going out to dinner with the boss. Travis looked at her with hunger in his eyes, but she still had a very hard time believing that a man like him actually wanted her, or why he actually did. Maybe he was as lonely as she was sometimes. Even when she'd been engaged to Rick, she'd felt alone. She just hadn't really had time to think about it then.

Fingering the chain around her neck as she walked carefully down the stairs, her heart lightened as she thought about Travis and the faith he'd had in her when he'd given her the unicorn. She wouldn't—she couldn't—make too much out of the attention Travis was giving her. While it might be good for her ego, there couldn't possibly be anything more to his behavior than to lighten her spirits, and maybe a misplaced sense of responsibility for their accident in the parking lot. Men like Travis Harrison weren't interested in women like her. Yeah. Maybe he would screw her if he was in-between women, but having a brief affair with him wouldn't be good for her. It would leave her feeling even more empty when it was over. She needed to remember that.

The doorbell rang and her eyes flew to the clock. He was twenty-five minutes early. Her pulse accelerated as she walked to the door and grasped the handle, wondering if she really should have sent that picture of the red lingerie she was wearing. It had been an impulse, a rare mischievous moment for her. Now, she wondered what he'd say.

The face that greeted her was not the one she'd been expecting, and the slight smile on her lips turned to a frown as she saw her ex-fiancé standing on her doorstep in a pair of jeans and a t-shirt, looking more disheveled than she'd ever seen him. Ally took in his light brown hair and even features, waiting for the emotions she should be feeling to register. But she felt...nothing.

"What do you want?" she asked him calmly, wanting nothing more than for him to leave.

"I want to come back, Ally." Rick sent her a tormented look.

"No," she answered simply. Did he seriously think she'd even consider it? She might be codependent, but she wasn't *that* damn pathetic.

He walked around her and into the foyer. "You got me fired. I think you at least owe me a place to stay."

Ally closed the door and faced him. "I didn't get you fired. And you should be in jail for the money you charged to me after you screwed someone else in this house and we broke up."

"Bullshit. My boss knew exactly what happened. How would he know that? He didn't think it was appropriate behavior for a new professional in the practice. They're all family men. How would he have found out, if not for you? You, me, and Amber were the only ones who knew," Rick said bitterly.

Ally gritted her teeth. "Get out. Go stay with your new girlfriend. You're not staying here."

"Amber doesn't want me to stay with her. She said she's reconsidered our relationship and she broke up with me." His tone got whiney and less angry.

Maybe because you're a cheating bastard! Did his girlfriend even know, or had Rick made up some fantastic story that the woman had bought into because she was young and naïve? "Did she know we were engaged?"

"I'd told her we were having problems. We were, Ally. You were gaining weight, and you came home every night smelling like alcohol, grease, and cigarettes from the bar. It wasn't exactly good for our romantic relationship. You never had time for me. I needed you, but you were never there. So I slipped up. I know I shouldn't have done it, but we were together five years. Do you really want to give all that up for one mistake? We should try again." His blue eyes weren't pleading or remorseful. His look was calculated and so were his words. "I was going to pay you back. I needed something to get me through until I started getting paid. I'd been thinking about us anyway. I think we could have worked everything out. We planned for years. It just got too hard having you gone all the time."

Bastard! He'd needed the money to buy things to impress his new woman. No doubt he hadn't thought for even a second about her until his girlfriend started having second thoughts. He'd all but admitted that.

She took a long, hard look at Rick. He was physically attractive, but the sight of him made her guts churn. This man, this unfaithful jerk, had been her whole life for years. Now, he wanted her to take him back? He wasn't just an ass; he was sociopathic. "So you came running back here until you find another job and another woman to screw?"

"Ally, I need you. I didn't realize how much until I didn't have you anymore." His eyes roamed her face and body. "You look good. Have you lost weight?"

She clenched her fists, trying desperately not to let him get to her. This man had been her life, her reason for existing, until he'd ruined everything.

He's trying to make you feel guilty. He's trying to get to you, make you feel like he's justified because of your behavior.

Maybe she hadn't been there every time he needed her, but she'd been working for them. "I worked my ass off for you, Rick. And I'm not responsible for you losing your job. And yeah, I let my appearance go because I needed sleep more than I needed a haircut or a manicure. And yeah, I gained a few pounds because I didn't have time to work out or watch my diet. I was too busy worrying about you and what you wanted."

"Ally, I regret—"

She held up her hand to silence him. "The only thing I regret is wasting five years of my life on you." She yanked on the door and pulled it wide open. "Now get the hell out of my house."

Rick shot her an angry look, no longer hiding behind his remorseful façade. "You'll regret this, Ally. We built a life together. You were trying to get me back by making me lose my position. But I'll get another one, and you'll hate yourself for not giving us another chance."

"Get out," she spat out angrily, her hand on the doorknob trembling.

Rick slowly walked out the door, shooting her a murderous expression. "You're throwing everything away. Everything we worked so hard to get. You're not so young anymore, and you've never been exactly beautiful. I was the most successful guy you were ever going to find."

Ally slammed the door and bolted it, the wood hitting him in the ass on his way out the door. She just stood there for a moment, her whole body quaking with anger.

Why did his barbs still hurt? She didn't feel anything but loathing for him anymore, but her mind was plagued with doubts.

You gained weight.

You never had time for me.

You've never been exactly beautiful.

I needed you. You never had time for me.

Rationally, she knew he was an asshole, but for some reason, his negative words still made her stomach roll.

One tear rolled down her cheek, and then another. And she wasn't even sure why she was crying. Maybe it was because of the empty years she'd been with Rick, or maybe it was because of his manipulative comments meant to hurt her enough to take him back.

She sat on the couch, trying to make sense of her jumbled thoughts. She'd gone from her verbally abusive alcoholic mother to Rick, and she could hear both of their voices in her head. Her mother hadn't ever really had anything nice to say when she wasn't in a comatose state, rambling on about how her father had died, leaving her with an unappreciative, ugly child to feed. Ally knew they were the ramblings of a bitter alcoholic, but they'd still shaped the way she felt about herself. And then she'd met Rick, and although he hid his criticism beneath a veneer of manipulation, his veiled disparagement had hurt just as badly.

Had she wanted to be loved so desperately that she'd been willing to take what Rick had to offer because it was better than nothing?

A strangled sob left Ally's mouth, her tears falling more readily. Really, it all boiled down to the fact that she *had* wanted to be loved. "He never loved me," she whispered in an anguished voice. "And I don't think I ever loved him." Rick had used her, and in a way, she'd used him, too. She'd wanted to fill the aching loneliness inside her, and she'd fooled herself into believing that if she worked hard enough, if she gave up enough for Rick, he'd love her. "I'm a stupid, stupid woman." She hadn't loved Rick either. She'd just convinced herself that she did because maybe he was right. Maybe she had felt he was the best she'd ever get or that he was all she deserved.

Ally was openly sobbing when the doorbell rang. Choking back her emotions, she hastily swiped her palms over her cheeks, trying to hide her tears.

Travis.

Any excitement she'd felt earlier about an evening with her boss had fled. She didn't want to go out with him. She didn't want to see anyone. All she needed was some time to get herself together again. Seeing Rick had left her a mess, emotionally vulnerable. There was no way she could face Travis right now. Her emotions were too close to the surface.

She went to the door, but she didn't open it. Checking the peephole, she could see Travis's face. "I have to cancel for tonight. I'm not feeling well," she called through the door in the calmest voice possible. "I'm sorry."

"Are you sick?" Travis's low baritone sounded concerned. "Open the door, Alison."

"Can't. I might be contagious. I'll call you when I'm feeling better." Her voice trembled, and she cursed herself for allowing her anxiety to creep into her tone.

"You're upset. Open the door now," Travis demanded. "I'm not leaving until I see if you're okay."

Dammit. Why did Travis have to be so damned persistent? And stubborn! "Why can't you just go away? I don't want to see anyone right now." Her desperation to get rid of him made her break her pretense of being ill.

"You're not sick. You're upset. Open the door or I'll break a window," Travis threatened ominously.

Problem was, Ally knew Travis never made empty threats, and the last thing she wanted was to replace a window. He'd do it without a thought. Part of her was angry because he was threatening her, but another part was touched because it appeared like he genuinely cared. None of this was Travis's fault. The least she could do was face him, let him know she was okay.

After swiping a hand over her face one more time, she unbolted the door. If he was satisfied that she was fine, he'd go. She swung the door open and the worried expression on his face made her want to throw herself into his arms and cry until her emotions were spent. But instead, she turned her head and told him weakly, "I'm fine. I've had a bad day. I'm sorry you had to drive all the way over here."

Travis easily muscled his way past her and closed the door. He tipped her chin up and assessed her for several seconds before he spoke. "You've been crying. What happened? There's no problem big enough to make you cry. I can fix it."

Ally looked at him then, her eyes sweeping over his immaculate suit and tie. When her gaze landed on his face, she was taken aback by the fierceness of his expression. But that was Travis. He was a fixer of problems, big and small. Unfortunately, he couldn't fix her emotional turmoil or her dysfunctional mind. "Rick was here. He wants to get back together." She pulled away from him and walked into the living room, needing to get away from the temptation of telling him everything. "We argued. It just left me a little shaken up. I'll be fine." She would be okay. As soon as she could manage to bury her feelings of worthlessness and guilt deep enough where no one could see them.

Travis caught her around the waist and turned her to face him. "Did he hurt you? Did he touch you? If he did, I swear I'll kill him."

"No. We just had a disagreement. It was nothing really," she answered, trying to keep her voice calm.

Travis grasped her by the shoulders. "What happened? Tell me you didn't consider for even a moment taking that bastard back again," he said huskily, notes of both demand and desperation in his voice.

"I'm not. I wouldn't. It's just…" Her voice trailed off, Ally feeling at a loss as to how to explain. Tears started to form again, the droplets trickling down her cheeks in frustration and pain.

Travis swept her up in his arms and sat on the couch, keeping her on his lap. "Tell me." His voice was low and persuasive, his arms comforting.

Ally snapped like a broken tree branch dangling in the wind that had finally given way to the pressure and had fallen to the ground. She told Travis everything between broken sobs, purging herself of the emotions that had been plaguing her for so long. After she told him about her unwanted encounter with Rick, she explained how her mother had been while she was growing up and how inadequate she'd always felt.

"Why can't I stop hearing her voice in my head? She's been dead for years," Ally finished, frustrated with herself.

"Maybe because you chose the asshole as the next voice in your head. Did you think he was all you deserved, Ally? A man who would work you to death, treat you like shit, and manipulate the hell out of you?" Travis asked, every muscle in his body tense. "I know how fucking hard it is to not believe everything you're told and taught growing up. But believe me when I say that you don't deserve what you've gotten."

Ally looked up at Travis, his jaw clenched and his eyes wild with anger. "How did you do it, Travis? How did you live through what you had handed to you in your life and not be affected by it?" He'd grown up with a madman, and some of the experiences he'd shared with her made her shudder.

He tucked a lock of hair gently behind her ear as he answered, "I didn't. It affected me. But I had Mia and Kade. We all knew what was happening wasn't normal. And I grew up while I was in college. I had to. My father wasn't able to run the company anymore. The minute I finished school, I had him ousted for incompetency and took his place. Harrison was starting to flounder, and there were too many people counting on us to provide a living for them. The company wasn't going to withstand his insane behavior and erratic decision-making much longer."

"Did it make you feel vindicated? Were you free?" she asked quietly.

"It didn't hurt," Travis admitted. "I didn't do it for revenge. I did it to save the company my grandfather busted his ass to build. But I won't say part of me wasn't satisfied that I was finally able to strip my father of the power he'd had over all of us for our entire life."

"When did you stop being afraid of him?" Ally queried curiously.

"As soon as I got big enough to kick his ass," Travis replied, his hand absently stroking her hair. "He was the monster who had terrified every one of us for years. I finally realized when I finished high school that I didn't have to be afraid of him anymore. When Kade and I left for college, I warned him if he ever laid a hand on Mia or my mother again, I'd kill him."

"Did you kick his ass?" she asked hesitantly.

Travis shrugged. "I didn't have to. By then, he was nothing but a shell with an insane mind. But he never touched Mia after that. Or my mother…until he actually killed her."

"Would you have done it if you'd needed to?"

"Yes," Travis answered immediately. "I would have done anything to keep him from hurting the rest of my family."

Ally reached out her hand and stroked his cheek, letting her fingers wander into his hair. "You were so incredibly brave. I know everything you went through had to be painful, yet you survived intact."

Travis barked out an unamused laugh. "Maybe not intact, but yes, I survived."

"I'm sorry I had another meltdown on you." Ally felt a little silly now. After all that Travis had gone through in his lifetime, her history was mild in comparison.

"Don't," Travis said huskily, his arm tightening around her waist. "Don't minimize your emotions or push them under your skin. Stop being so damn hard on yourself. It's not your fault, Ally."

Ally took a deep breath, her gaze clashing with Travis's. "I need to get my shit together."

Travis rose, taking her with him. "You need to start listening to new voices. And add your own, too."

"I'll try," Ally told him adamantly, determined to break out of her old habits.

"You look beautiful, Ally." He took a step back. "Now take off your dress."

Ally's eyes shot to Travis's face, his intense, unrelenting stare making her take a step back. "What?" She knew she couldn't have heard him correctly.

"Take. Off. The. Dress. Either take it off willingly or I'll do it for you, and it probably won't be wearable anymore after I do," he growled.

"W-why?" She *had* heard him correctly, and her entire body flooded with heat.

"Because you're going to start to hear a new voice, and that voice is going to be mine while I make you come." Travis folded his arms in front of him and waited.

Chapter 10

Ally balked as she looked at Travis waiting arrogantly, expectantly. "I'm not taking off my dress. And you're not going to rip it. It probably cost a fortune." She crossed her arms in front of her, the two of them having a stare-down.

"You will," Travis remarked ominously as he slowly unbuttoned his suit jacket and shrugged it off his shoulders. "I didn't come here tonight to fuck you, Ally. But I'm going to because I can't wait any longer." His fingers went to the knot in his tie, and he nimbly unfastened it and slid it from around his neck. "And I don't think you want to wait any longer either." He started unbuttoning his pristine shirt. "I've waited four goddamn years, and there wasn't a single one of those days that my cock wasn't hard for you, that I didn't want to sink into you and make you mine." He unbuttoned the small fastenings at his cuffs and let the shirt slide off his shoulders, landing in a heap at his feet along with his jacket and tie. "Tonight you're mine. Completely. Unequivocally. You won't be hearing any other voice except mine telling you how damn beautiful you are, how much I want you. And you won't be feeling anything except pleasure."

Ally froze, gaping as she watched Travis's ripped abs and muscular arms being exposed to her hungry eyes. Sweet baby Jesus, the man was beautiful. He was all predatory grace and solid flesh that her fingers itched to touch. "You've been attracted to me for that long?"

He stalked her, moving the few steps necessary to pull her body into his. Lowering his head, he traced her sensitive earlobe with his tongue. "Not attracted, Ally. Obsessed," he answered harshly, his warm breath wafting over her ear.

Ally shivered, unable to stop herself from putting her hands to his chest, her fingers exploring silken skin over steely muscles. He had a tattoo, a beautiful phoenix flying free of fire on the right side of his chest, which just made him even hotter, more unpredictable. Travis was the last man on earth she could see with a tat. She smoothed down his ripped abdomen and up his back, savoring the feel of his heated skin beneath her fingers.

Travis nipped at the sensitive skin of her neck as he said huskily, "Time's up on the dress, sweetheart."

Ally jerked back as she felt his fists tighten on the material. "No! Don't." She wasn't sure if her concern was actually the dress. Really, for the first time in her life, she wanted to be sexually bold. She could see the desire in Travis's eyes, and she needed to trust it. Reaching up and behind her, she lowered the short zipper and started wriggling the material over her head, revealing the risqué underwear as the silken material moved upward. She was breathless with anxiety by the time she dropped the dress to the floor, standing right in front of Travis in nothing but tiny red panties, a matching bra, a garter belt, and silky stockings. Her stiletto heels were still on her feet, but they barely helped, as Travis was still towering over her.

He must have been holding his breath, and it released in a hiss before he said low and reverently, "My fantasies didn't come any-where close to imagining how sexy and beautiful you really are. Christ! How could you not know how hot you are, Ally?"

White-hot bolts of heat streaked through her core, drenching her panties as she watched the torment on Travis's face, sensed the feral hunger that was almost palpable in the air around them.

Travis finally stepped forward, lowering the straps on the bra to move his mouth over the skin of her shoulders. He unfastened the catch and slid the garment down her arms, careful of the patches of skin that were still healing. He palmed her breasts, his touch becoming rough and possessive and he watched his fingers play with her nipples, grunting with satisfaction as they hardened to painfully sensitive peaks. "Mine," he rumbled. "Beautiful and mine."

Ally moaned as he pinched and rolled each tip, his fingers exploring every inch of her breasts like he wanted to own them. "Travis," she gasped as he slid one hand behind her neck and took her mouth, plastering their bodies together. Ally opened to him, his demanding tongue piercing between her lips in a blatant act of possession. The feel of being skin-to-skin with Travis was exquisite and sensual, her nipples rubbing against his rock-hard chest as he devoured her mouth with erotic strokes of his tongue. He grasped her ass and pulled her flush against him, her pussy flooding at the feel of his enormous erection pressing against her pelvis. She wrapped her arms around his neck and surrendered, her hands stroking down his back as she melted into him.

Travis's mouth left hers, sliding down her shoulders, his mouth latching onto one of her nipples, sucking and licking it thoroughly before moving to the other. He crouched lower, landing on his knees, his tongue tracing a line slowly down to her panties. "I'm going to make you come with my mouth first, Ally. And then I'm going to fuck you and make you come again," he said in a low, dangerous voice that was slightly muffled against her lower belly.

Ally looked down at him and the sight of his dark head so close to her pussy nearly made her come just from the erotic image. She put her hands on his shoulders as he gripped her panties and tore them from her body with a violent tug. It was the hottest thing she'd ever seen, and Travis's desire for her was overwhelming her. She was lost as he grasped her hips hard, parting her legs wide with a hard nudge of his thigh, and burying his face and mouth into her bared mound.

Travis wasn't gentle or teasing. He used his mouth and tongue to forcefully part her folds, his fiery tongue landing on her clit almost immediately. The tiny bundle of nerves responded, the bud hard and sensitive, reacting to every strong stroke of his tongue. He drank from her pussy like it was nectar, his tongue moving hard against her clit, driving her higher and higher, making her desperation even greater than his.

"Oh, God. Yes," she whimpered, her nails biting into his shoulders. "Travis, please." Ally's entire body quivered, the heat starting in her belly and shooting straight to her pussy.

Travis plundered without mercy, without pause, his whiskered jaw abrading her inner thighs, an erotic sensation that made her spear her hands into his hair and hold his head against her, a silent plea for more.

His teeth nipped her clit, his tongue flicking relentlessly, harder and harder.

Ally came apart with a tortured moan. "Travis," she groaned, gripping his scalp tighter, holding him against her pussy as her body bucked and splintered into tiny pieces.

She gasped as he continued to lap at her folds, prolonging the exquisite pleasure, as though he was desperately parched and needed to get every drop.

Ally would have collapsed to the floor had Travis not straightened and grasped her around the waist, holding her tightly as he kissed her, allowing her to taste herself on his mouth. The embrace was heady and intoxicating, a new experience since Rick had supposedly hated performing that particular act on a woman, so she'd never experienced it. He'd been her only lover...until now.

Ally fumbled between their bodies, trying to undo Travis's belt, desperate to give him the same magnificent pleasure that he'd just lavished on her.

Yanking his mouth away from hers, Travis grasped her wrist. "Don't," he rasped. "If you put those beautiful lips around my cock, I won't last more than five seconds." He stepped back, his heated stare never leaving her as he stripped off his shoes and socks, shucking his pants and his boxer briefs down his legs and kicking out of them.

"God, you're magnificent." Ally couldn't stop herself from letting her eyes roam his sculpted body, her gaze landing on his enormous, engorged cock. His nude body took her breath away. She licked her lips sensually, eager to taste him.

"Fuck, Ally! Don't do that. There's only so much I can take," Travis demanded, grasping her by the hand and leading her to a waist-high table where she had her plants and knickknacks. He placed her palms on the table, making her bend over. "Right now all I need is to fuck you." His hands cupped her ass, gripping the cheeks and stroking. "Do you have any idea how this ass has tortured me over the last four years?"

She didn't, but hearing the longing in his tone made her shiver. "No," she answered tremulously.

"Do you know how much I want you, Ally?" He slipped his hand between her thighs, sliding a teasing finger through her wetness.

"I think so," she answered on a moan. Probably as much as she needed him right now.

He leaned forward, covering her body with his, his mouth beside her ear. "I want you so much that I can barely breathe. I've wanted you for years. You're hearing *my* voice, now. Can you understand how beautiful you are to me?"

Ally could feel his erect cock between her thighs as he pulled his fingers away and she gripped it. "I want you, too."

"Not nearly as much as I want you," he told her huskily. "You're going to be mine now, Ally. I'll sate you until you don't want anyone else. Nobody will ever need you like I do. Nobody will ever pleasure you like I will."

"Travis, please," Ally begged, needing him inside her right now.

He grasped a handful of her hair and pulled her head up. "Look at yourself. Tell me you see yourself as beautiful right now."

Ally met her own face in the oval mirror in front of her, her face ravaged with desire. Her eyes met Travis's in the mirror, his expression raw and feral. At that moment, he looked beautiful in his unveiled need, and it made her feel the same way. "I look like I need to get fucked," she told him breathlessly. She didn't really recognize the dazed and wild woman staring back at her.

"Yeah. You need me inside you. And that's the most gorgeous thing I've ever seen," Travis told her hoarsely.

He held her gaze as he thrust into her, burying himself to his balls with a groan. Ally let out a cry of relief as he filled her, stretched her until she could feel nothing but him. Travis was mastering her body, filling her senses, and she was barely keeping her sanity. "Oh, God," she moaned, unable to form any coherent thoughts.

"You feel so fucking good, Ally. Tell me what you want," he demanded.

"You. Just you," she answered on a pant, moaning as Travis pulled almost entirely out of her and stroked back inside again, filling every empty space inside her.

He pumped his hips again. "You want me to make you come, Ally?" His harsh voice sounded next to her ear.

"Yes, Travis. Please."

"Ask for it. Take whatever you need from me. You deserve to be pleasured. Do you understand?"

"Yes. Yes." Travis made her feel like she deserved the world. "Let me come. I want it. I want you," she said greedily, her body feeling like she was ready to come apart.

"That's right, sweetheart. Be demanding. Take the pleasure you deserve." Travis straightened, keeping his eyes on her face as they stared at each other in a daze in the mirror. "Keep looking at me. Don't stop." He let go of her hair and grasped her hips, his cock slamming into her over and over as he grasped her hip with one hand and slid the other down her abdomen, his finger sliding into her wetness.

Ally watched Travis's face, mesmerized, his expression alternating between agony and ecstasy as he buried himself inside her again and again. She moaned as he teased her clit, her eyes momentarily fluttering shut from sensation overload as she thrust her hips back to meet every stroke of his cock, burying him even deeper.

"Look at me, Ally. Come for me. I want to watch you. Give in to this. Give in to me. Let go."

It was too much. She opened her eyes and was speared by Travis's intense, commanding look. He hammered into her ruthlessly, and her climax ripped through her, every nerve ending pulsating as she screamed. "Travis!"

"You'll always be mine," Travis groaned as he leaned his body over hers again. Moving her hair to the side, his mouth suckled at the back of her neck before he gave her a sensual bite that made her squeal.

It wasn't enough to break Ally's skin, but the carnality of the action intensified her orgasm until the inner walls of her channel clenched and released tightly around Travis's cock, as though it wanted to keep him impaled inside her forever.

Ally's elbows gave way and her head landed on top of her arms as she watched Travis's head fall back, the muscles in his neck flexing as he groaned, flooding her womb with his warm release as he held her hips tightly against him. "Mine," he growled, wrapping his arms around her body and pulling her up and back to rest against him. He stepped back and collapsed on the couch, bringing her down on top of him, breaking her fall. Turning her body so they were chest to chest, he wrapped his arms around her, their legs entangled, her head on his shoulder.

Ally panted as she relished the uneven rise and fall of Travis's breath, knowing he'd been just as affected by what had just happened as she had been. "You just rocked my world, Mr. Harrison," she said breathlessly. Never in her wildest imaginings could she ever have seen her solemn, no-nonsense boss as a dominant, passionate, intense lover.

His hand connected with her ass with a loud *smack*. It stung, but it didn't really hurt.

"*Travis*," he insisted. "Mr. Harrison applies to more than one person. I don't want you forgetting who just fucked you half senseless."

He'd actually screwed her completely senseless, but she answered saucily. "Did you? I didn't notice."

He slapped her ass again. "You noticed. And you're going to keep on noticing until the only voice you hear is mine telling you how much I want to fuck you."

Ally speared a hand in his hair, stroking the thick strands between her fingers. "Thank you. I've never felt that way before," she told him seriously.

"How?"

"Sexy. Wanted. Beautiful," she admitted quietly. "I'll never forget this night."

"No, you won't. Because we'll be doing it every damn night," Travis rasped. "I meant what I said, Ally. You're mine now. I'm not letting you go."

Oh, God. Ally wanted to be his, but she was trying to set herself free, not set herself up for another heartbreak. Travis Harrison might want her right now, and he'd helped her just by giving her a taste—okay, maybe a feast—of desire. But she was his employee, his assistant. "Travis, I'm your employee. We can't just continue to have an affair."

Travis sat up, causing Ally to have to straddle him. "The hell we can't. And it isn't an affair. It isn't like either one of us is attached."

"Then what would you call it?" Ally asked curiously.

"A goddamn fantasy that's actually coming true," Travis told her obstinately.

"And when the fantasy ends?" Ally shot back at him.

"It won't. Not ever," Travis told her stubbornly. "Christ! If you could spend five years with a man who didn't give a rat's ass about you, why can't you try being with a man who cares about you and what you want?"

Ally looked at Travis's face, the hurt in his eyes flooring her. "I'm sorry. I guess with you I'd just be waiting until the novelty of screwing your secretary wore off and I'd be hurt again. It's not you. It's me, Travis. I'm scared to try again so soon."

"I'd die before I'd hurt you, Ally," he told her huskily, his hand stroking her back absently.

An enormous lump lodged in her throat, as she suddenly considered *why* she wouldn't give whatever was happening between her and Travis a chance to grow. Did she think she didn't deserve a guy who cared? Did she think Travis didn't really care? Whatever her reasoning, it was self-destructive and ridiculous. He was a man like any other. Yes…he was one of the wealthiest men in the world, but to judge him solely based on that fact was just plain stupid. She knew now that he was a good man beneath his gruff, solemn exterior. And she already cared about him. And he'd showed her more concern than any other person in her life ever had. Maybe that was the really scary part. "I guess I'm just not used to someone who cares. But I'd like to get used to it," she admitted hesitantly. And she wanted to care about Travis in return. He needed to lighten up, and whether he'd admit it or not, he needed someone who cared about *him* and not his bottom line. And that was something she could and would give him.

Getting him to open up to her wouldn't be easy, and she wouldn't have an easy time being vulnerable to him. But couldn't it end up being worth the risk? Ally lifted a hand and stroked his rough jawline. "Will you let me care about you, Travis?" She held her breath, terrified by leaving herself raw and vulnerable to this man, but wanting him too badly not to take the risk.

He caught her hand in his and kissed her palm. "Care, Ally. I need you."

Ally let out her breath, relief flooding her body. In opening herself up to Travis, she'd unwittingly allowed him to reveal his vulnerability to her. For a proud, intensely alpha male like Travis, his risk was as big as her own. "I'm afraid it's too late to start. I already do care," she whispered softly.

His dark eyes pinned her with a possessive look, but something miraculous happened at the same time. For the first time since Ally had known him, Travis Harrison gave her the happiest, sincerest, and broadest smile she'd ever seen, and she knew she was completely lost. And, seeing his handsome, almost boyish expression, Ally decided he was definitely worth the risk.

Chapter 11

"That necklace looks beautiful on you, Ally," Mia Hamilton said sincerely, her eyes staring at Ally across the table of the casual family restaurant.

All four sets of female eyes at the table flew to Ally, murmuring their agreement appreciatively. "Where did you get it?" Maddie asked curiously.

Ally squirmed in her seat, fingering the lovely unicorn necklace that she hadn't removed since the day Travis had given it to her. The last week had been the happiest of her life, and not a night had gone by that Travis hadn't been in her bed. He'd gone to work late every single day for the last week, grumbling that he couldn't wait until she came back to work on Thursday. Travis filled her days with laughter with his naughty and thoughtful antics, and her nights with dark desire that never went unsated.

"It was a gift from Travis," Mia answered for Ally before she could decide what to say.

"Wow. It's beautiful." Asha reached out, brushing Ally's fingers aside to examine the small unicorn.

"It was a birthday gift," Ally murmured. Looking at Mia, she asked, "How did you know?"

Mia took a sip of her water and set it back down before answering. "Because I made it. Travis picked the stones and what I needed to craft it. And he gave me very little time to do it because he wanted you to have it that day."

Ally gaped at Mia. The necklace she was wearing was a Mia Hamilton design? "I thought he just picked it up somewhere."

Mia chuckled. "He did. My studio. He couldn't find exactly what he wanted, so I had to make it for him. Those are the finest quality gems available. And he drew exactly what he wanted, so it wasn't difficult to design since he did most of the work for me. He knew exactly how it needed to be. It's unique. The unicorn must have significance. Why?"

Ally's heart raced, the thought of Travis going to all that trouble and expense just to get her an exact replica of her fantasy unicorn making the piece of jewelry just that much more precious to her. "I write as a hobby. He liked the first story and the unicorn is one of the characters. He wants me to finish the books."

"And will you?" Kara Hudson asked from her seat next to Asha. "It's a very romantic gesture."

"Definitely." Maddie nodded from across the table.

"Travis has been different lately. He actually kissed me back on the cheek when I kissed him good-bye yesterday. And he's smiling. Not that cynical, obnoxious expression he gets, but actually smiling. I was thinking he must be getting laid." Asha gave Ally a sly look. "Am I right?"

"Oh my God!" Mia squealed. "You and Travis have been burning up the sheets? I should have known when he was in such a panic about the necklace. But I thought you were engaged?"

Ally hadn't really had a chance to tell any of the women that she wasn't engaged anymore. Only Asha knew. She explained what had happened with Rick and that she was no longer engaged, but she didn't mention Travis. Maybe because the relationship was so new that she couldn't really explain what they were to each other.

"Snake!"

"Asshole!"

"Slimy bastard!"

"Dickhead!"

Each woman interjected a derogatory name for Rick as Ally explained.

"So you're free, and Travis pounced. Smart man, my brother," Mia said with a smile as she took a huge bite of her club sandwich.

Ally shook her head. "I wouldn't say he pounced exactly."

"How long did it take him to get you into bed?" Asha asked, amused. "He's had it bad for you for years."

"Who says I slept with him?" Ally said with false indignation. "Maybe we're just becoming friends."

"Bullshit," Kara remarked as she popped a fry into her mouth. "You haven't denied it, so that means you definitely did him."

"Travis is hot, but he's always been so dark and broody. But I bet that makes him good in the sack?" Maddie said thoughtfully.

"Stop!" Mia held up her hand. "There's an 'ick' factor for me here. He's my brother. I absolutely do not want to know if he's a good lay."

All the women laughed uproariously, and Ally smiled.

Mia lowered her hand and leaned slightly across the table and asked in a loud whisper, "But *did* you do him?"

There was something really embarrassing about being questioned about her sex life by the sister of the man who rocked her world every time he touched her, so she merely nodded reluctantly.

"Oh, thank God," Mia answered, straightening up to continue her lunch. "No wonder he's smiling."

"We aren't really serious," Ally told Mia nervously. "I mean, we're just dating, getting to know each other."

"Carnally," Asha added with a smirk.

Ally elbowed her friend lightly. "It's nothing serious."

Mia's brows narrowed and her eyes danced with mischief. "You don't know Travis well enough then. Even when he was a boy, if he decided he wanted something, he got it. He's annoyingly persistent when he covets anything. He'll have a ring on your finger within a month."

"I don't think he's like that with me. I'm sure he won't," Ally denied, embarrassed.

"He will," Asha agreed with Mia ominously.

"Do you care for him, Ally?" Mia asked, concerned.

"I do. Probably more than I should at this stage of our relationship," Ally admitted, knowing she was beginning to care way too much, too fast. "I'm just a little scared. I just got out of a bad relationship."

"Travis isn't like that, Ally," Mia replied softly. "When he cares, he cares deeply. His affections might not be easily gained, but once you have them, he'll never betray you. And he wanted the unicorn for you to show he cares because he isn't good at giving or receiving affection. Honestly, I've actually never seen him care about a woman this way, and I knew when he finally fell, he'd fall hard. Please don't hurt him. No one deserves to be loved more than Travis. And when it's the right woman, he'll love her obsessively and forever. It's just the way he's made."

Ally's heart squeezed inside her chest, knowing she'd give anything to be that woman. In the week since she and Travis had first made love, his affection was already changing her, making her hear his voice inside her head instead of all the negative things she'd always believed about herself. "I wish I could give him something," she mused quietly, thinking about his unrelenting support, his faith in her.

"I think you already have," Asha assured Ally. "He's happy."

Mia nodded her agreement and the group of women launched into more general conversation. The lunch was a totally enjoyable interlude, and Ally had fun getting to know Maddie and Kara better. It was obvious to her that all the women at the table loved their alpha male husbands to death, even though they good-naturedly complained about them being overprotective and overbearing at times.

Ally's phone pinged in her purse as they were getting up to go their separate ways. Pulling it out, she smiled as she saw the text message from Travis:

I need to get rid of this damn desk!

He'd complained more than once how the desk distracted him, about the images he had throughout the day. Her heart flip-flopped at the thought, that she could actually be a distraction to a man as driven as Travis Harrison.

She said her good-byes to all the women, promising to become one of the regular members of their lunch club. Once she reached her car, she leaned up against it and texted:

As your assistant, it's my job to find you a new one then, Mr. Harrison.

It only took a moment to get a reply:

Like hell you will. Nobody else is using this desk. I guess I'll just be a masochist. How is your day?

She already knew he'd vehemently refuse to get rid of it, but she laughed out loud anyway before replying:

Good. Just had lunch with the girls. How about you?

He answered simply:

I miss you.

Ally's heart melted, and she traced the words on her phone with a sigh. When Travis said or did things like that, her whole being ached for him. Travis wasn't a demonstrative or bullshitting type of guy. Those words were sincere, an expression of his emotions at that moment, and she cherished them because she knew he didn't express himself lightly.

She answered:

I miss you, too. I'll make you dinner.

His answer came quickly:

I'd be happier if you'd actually be my dinner.

Ally barely stifled a moan at that thought. She needed to fan herself, and it wasn't because of the humidity and heat of the Florida sun. There was nothing hotter than Travis's demanding, bossy, alpha ways in the bedroom, and the way he mastered her body. But she answered him cheekily:

I offer to cook for you and all you want is sex?

It took a few minutes to get his reply:

I want a whole lot more than sex. And women don't usually cook for me. Thank you, Ally. I'll see you around six.

She frowned at his response, wondering exactly what he meant. Women didn't cook for him? No…they probably didn't. He did most things alone, and if and when he did have a date, she was pretty certain the woman would expect the finest from Travis Harrison. Did he actually think she'd been chastising him? She'd just been playing with him. She didn't question whether or not he was using her anymore just for sex, and his answer had sounded rather remorseful. And for the very first time she realized that "thank you" was actually in his vocabulary. And it touched her that he was thanking her for something so very simple. She didn't want to see him be sorry for joking around with her. Truth was, she loved seeing him fun and playful, and his dirty talk always turned her on. It was doubtful that anyone else saw him that way. She answered:

Six is fine. And if you get here early, I'll be your appetizer. But I will feed you. You'll need the energy.

She held her breath, hoping he'd come back with a playful response. The last thing she ever wanted to do was crush Travis's playfulness because he had taken her comment seriously. He was already too solemn, too serious, and his lighter side was something she wanted to see more of.

He replied:

If I didn't have a meeting, I'd be in my car right fucking now.

Ally let out a relieved laugh and typed:

No need. I have to cook. But it's warm today. I think I might have to cook naked. Think about that in your meeting. Hope it goes well.

Her reply came almost instantly:

You'll pay for that, woman!

Smiling, she returned:

I'm counting on it, handsome. See you later.

Ally put her phone back in her purse and opened the door of her vehicle. She drove to the grocery store to pick up what she needed to make Travis a nice dinner, her heart lighter than it had been for as long as she could remember.

She's mine!

Travis clenched his phone tightly, staring at the words Ally had texted.

She misses me.

He thought he'd majorly fucked up by making her think he just wanted to fuck her. Well...he *did* want to fuck her. Every damn minute of the day. But Travis knew his physical desire was just a product of how much he wanted her to belong to him. He felt like a caveman, the desire to drag her off to his isolated cave where no one would ever take her from him almost unbearable.

He leaned back in his chair and closed his eyes, images of the time he'd spent with Ally during the last week floating through his mind. He'd now been the object of several of her sweet, warm smiles, and every one of them had hit him like a boulder to the gut. Oh, it wasn't like they still didn't argue—like the argument they'd had over the wardrobe he'd provided for her. He'd settled it by taking all the clothing upstairs and putting it away, ignoring her while she systematically listed reasons why she couldn't accept them. He'd won when he kissed her breathless and told her he'd probably tear them all off her eventually anyway. Damn, but his woman was stubborn. Travis wanted to give her the world, but she wouldn't let him.

If she knew everything about me, would she still want to be with me?

Chances were, she'd run like hell, and he really wouldn't blame her. He'd shared a lot of things with Ally that he'd never shared with another soul. But there were a few things he just couldn't seem to tell her, too afraid she'd look at him in horror and run away. And Travis knew that would destroy him.

I need to just enjoy the time I have with her. Not think about the future right now.

Problem was, he wasn't the type of guy who just lived in the moment, and he needed Ally too badly to even contemplate her leaving him.

He opened his eyes, staring at the ceiling. Ally made him ecstatically happy, but more fiercely territorial than he'd thought he could ever possibly be. Luckily, she didn't seem to mind the fact that he always took her hard, fast and rough. In fact, she seemed to relish it. But he wanted even more. He wanted her complete submission to him, needed to know she was completely his, and he couldn't get his frenzied cravings for that under control. Did she know she had him completely by the balls every minute of every day and never let go?

I might have to cook naked.

Oh yeah, she definitely knew, and she did everything she could to make him crazy. He loved it and he hated it. It was almost like she wanted to see him break, go completely caveman on her.

"Sweetheart, you have no idea exactly how demanding I could really be with you," he whispered huskily, wanting to make her just as damn desperate as he was for her.

It wasn't that Travis didn't know that Ally was satisfied every time they were intimate. He made damn certain that she was. But he wanted her to let go completely, surrender herself totally to him and the white-hot passion that nearly consumed them both every time they were together. She was so fucking responsive, and she got so beautifully aroused. But he still felt like she was holding a part of herself back. And he was greedy. He wanted everything she had.

Glancing up at the clock, Travis cursed as he realized it was almost time for his meeting.

"Great," he whispered harshly. "I'll sit through the whole damn meeting wondering if Ally's really cooking naked, my dick so hard I won't be able to concentrate."

He got up from the chair and straightened his tie. He'd warned Ally that he'd make her pay for teasing him. Problem was, every damn time she touched him, he damn near lost it. Walking out of the office and toward his meeting, he smiled, thinking of a solution that could remedy that problem.

Chapter 12

Ally entered her bedroom, still damp and completely nude after her shower, squealing as the door of the bedroom closed loudly behind her. Relief flooded her body as she saw Travis standing in front of the closed door, still dressed in his office attire.

Needing to take a couple of deep breaths because of the scare he gave her by appearing out of nowhere, she flushed as his eyes roamed over her, his expression feral and hungry.

"You're early," she gasped, still not completely comfortable standing in front of Travis bare-assed naked. It was barely five o'clock, and she hadn't expected him this early. She'd given him a key to the house, but he usually didn't let himself in.

"I got extremely hungry for my appetizer," he replied huskily. "And I couldn't wait. Catching you at this moment is extremely convenient."

Ally shivered as she looked into his eyes. He seemed different tonight, almost dangerous. Not that she was afraid of him, her body reacting to his fierceness, his proprietary stare. "It is?" she answered innocently. It seemed like the more desperately Travis wanted her, the hotter she became.

"Very," he answered casually as he stripped off the jacket of his suit. "Do you know what it's like sitting through a meeting while visualizing you naked the entire time? I wasn't exactly productive. And I did warn you that you'd pay for your teasing."

He had. And there was nothing Ally wanted more than for him to take his revenge. "I'm sorry," she answered insincerely, because she really wasn't very sorry at all.

"Don't move," Travis commanded in a low and demanding voice. "That meeting was very uncomfortable, Ally. And I know what I'd usually do is fuck you senseless, but I'm not going to do that right now."

Ally was flooded with disappointment, followed by curiosity. She watched him warily as he slowly removed his black tie. "Then let me just grab a robe—"

"No." Travis moved then, not stopping until he was right in front of her. "I don't think so. I did promise I'd make you pay. The problem is that every time you touch me, I can't think straight and I end up fucking you hard and fast. Do you like that?"

Ally looked up at him, confused. "You know I do," she answered quietly.

"But I've never really gotten the chance to explore you, find out exactly what you like." He moved behind her, and before Ally knew what exactly he had in mind, he'd tightened his tie around her wrists. "The only way I can think of to not lose control is to keep you from touching me," he said mildly.

Ally yanked at her hands. They were bound together behind her back, not tight enough to hurt, but snugly enough so she couldn't move them. "Travis, what are you doing?"

"Making you pay first. And then finding out what you really like. Exploring you. Exploring your pleasure."

Ally felt a moment of panic as her vision went dark, and she could feel Travis tying something at the back of her head. "I can't see." The helplessness was both disconcerting and arousing.

Travis's arms came around her waist, pulling her back against him. "Do you trust me, Ally?" His hands roamed over her belly and up to cup her breasts. "You don't need to see. You just need to feel."

She relaxed back against his body, the feel of his clothed body against her back making her want to get him naked now. "I do trust you."

He pinched her breasts, bringing her already hard nipples to painfully sensitive diamond-hard peaks. His mouth explored her neck, nipping at the skin and stroking over it with his tongue. Her pussy flooded and she squirmed uncomfortably with a helpless moan. She was completely at Travis's mercy, and that sensation turned her on more than she ever thought possible.

"Do you know that the moment I got out of that meeting, I had to go get myself off, thinking about how I was going to get my revenge?" he asked her in a hoarse whisper, his warm breath caressing her ear.

Ally quivered at the thought of Travis stroking himself while thinking of her erotic torture. "I wish I could have watched," she admitted in a breathy voice, her lack of sight making her bolder.

Travis removed his arms and placed one hand on her neck, bending her body over. "It made me want to do this." He moved her bound hands aside with one hand and stroked her ass with the other.

Smack!

His hand connecting with the flesh of her ass jolted her. She'd been expecting him to take her from behind, and she'd been more than ready. But the sting of his hand on her sent a jolt of electricity through her entire body.

Smack!

He'd landed the second stroke before Ally came out of her erotic daze enough to realize he was actually spanking her.

"Are you going to play nice from now on?" Travis asked in a controlled voice.

Holy hell! Her ass tingled, but he wasn't hitting her hard enough to really hurt. It was more of an erotic sting. His dominance and control was arousing, seductive. "No," she answered boldly, wanting more.

Smack. Smack. Smack.

Every time his hand connected with her ass, she let out a gasping, needy moan. Sweet Jesus, being helpless to Travis, him being in total control of her body was about to make her come, and he'd hardly touched her. "Please," she rasped, desperate for him to take her now.

He stroked over her ass, and then between her thighs. "I guess you like being naughty. Christ! You're wet. Tell me what you like, Ally. What really turns you on?"

Anything with Travis, everything with Travis. "You. Everything you do." He was teasing her clit with his finger, gliding easily because she was so aroused. "It's all good. You're the first man who ever made me come. The first man who ever put his mouth on me. Everything you do makes me crazy."

He put an arm around her shoulders to steady her. "Is that really true?" He sounded angry and astounded.

"Yes. My ex was my first and only before you, and he never tasted me, never made me climax." Maybe it was because she couldn't see his face, or because her whole body was trembling with need, but she felt like she could tell him anything, everything.

"I like being your first." His finger increased its pressure on the bundle of nerves he was teasing, his other hand sliding down her back and down the curve of her ass. "Do you like this, being helpless, trusting me to pleasure you?"

"Yes," she answered with a throaty groan.

The hand on her butt moved between her legs, wetting his fingers in her moist pussy and moving back up sensually to the area between the cheeks of her ass, lubricating the area before gently moving his index finger into her anus.

Ally's body tensed, conflicted between the pleasure he was giving her by stroking her clit, and the apprehension of a forbidden sensation she'd never experienced before.

"Relax, sweetheart. I'm not going to hurt you. I'm just exploring," Travis crooned, pulling his finger out and then back in gently. "Does it hurt?"

It didn't, and Ally let herself relax, starting to enjoy the gentle in and out motion.

She almost whined in disappointment as he took his hand away from her pussy. But almost immediately, his mouth took the place of his fingers, and Ally knew he must have dropped to his knees.

Her head began to spin as he continued to glide his finger in and out of her ass, while his mouth and tongue devoured her pussy.

"Oh God. Travis. Please. I don't think I can take anymore." She was panting, trying to catch her breath as her climax built, Travis's heated, marauding tongue driving her insane. His erotic imprisonment made her arousal sharper, any inhibitions she'd ever had completely gone. There was only the pleasure washing over her body like a waterfall, pummeling at her until she no longer had a coherent thought.

Her climax tore through her body the moment Travis buried two of his fingers into her empty channel, her body so full of him that she imploded. Her channel clamped around his fingers, and Ally threw her head back and groaned. "Travis, Travis, Travis."

He was there to catch her before she hit the floor, her legs too weak to remain standing. Travis carried her, still trembling in the aftermath of her orgasm, to the bed and dropped her in the middle of it. She heard the rustling of his clothes as she panted, trying to recover her breath.

She let out an audible sigh as she felt his naked body come down over hers, the feel of his heated skin making her groan feebly. She felt the ties on her hands come loose, only to be fastened again over her head and obviously attached to the headboard. "Please. I need to touch you, Travis." She wanted to wrap her arms around his hot body, absorb his essence.

"Not this time. You look beautiful like this, Ally. I just want you to feel. I want this to last," he rumbled. "You might be the one bound, but I'm just as helpless as you are. I want you to need me as much as I need you."

Ally's heart raced, amazed that he just didn't understand that she did need him just as much as he needed her. "I do."

"Tell me what you want," he demanded, wrapping her legs around his waist.

"I want you to fuck me. Please. I need you."

Travis let out a low growl of satisfaction and teased her clit with the silky head of his hard cock. He rolled her nipples between his fingers, toying with them. "You're mine, Ally. Tell me you're mine."

"I'm all yours, Travis. And you're mine." Ally felt the same possessive instincts rising inside her, the need for him to belong to her as much as she belonged to him. "I want you to be mine. And I never want you touching another woman," she told him fiercely, lifting her hips up, begging him with her body to take her. "Now fuck me."

"Jesus, I love it when you say that," he rasped.

Ally never had a chance to ask him which part he liked. He impaled her swiftly and deeply, his cock sinking deep inside her, filling her. "Yes," she hissed. "Fuck me, Travis. I feel like I'm going to die if you don't."

She continued to babble encouragement, anything to try to make him understand that she had the same ferocious, carnal needs as he did.

Travis grasped her hips, starting with hard, deep strokes of his cock, each thrust ecstasy for her as he claimed her. "Mine," he grunted with every pump of his hips.

Ally was frenzied, her desperation to feel more of Travis making her crazy. She wrapped her bound hands around the tie and yanked, feeling the headboard yield and the cheap plywood slat give way. Her hands still bound together, she leaned up and looped them around Travis's neck, bringing him down on top of her, her lips searching for his mouth. "Kiss me," she panted, her patience at an end.

"Fuck it! I can't take it anymore. Touch me," Travis exclaimed irritably, his lips crashing down on hers and his cock beginning to pummel into her as they strained together.

Ally relished the feel of his body on hers, his demanding tongue invading her mouth. This is what she needed the most, this demanding, fervent passion that was about to make her come apart.

Tightening her legs around his hips, she demanded more, meeting Travis's every thrust with an urgency of her own.

She detonated, coming apart as she pulled her mouth from his, screaming his name as she came, her fingernails digging into his shoulders as her body pulsated.

"Oh, fuck yeah. Mark the shit out of me." Travis groaned carnally as his warm release flooded deep inside her.

He ripped the blindfold from her eyes, and tossed it to the floor, watching her shudder in the aftermath of her climax.

He rolled to her side, and quickly untied her hands. Ally wrapped her arms completely around him, plastering herself against the warmth of his body. As erotic as being bound and blinded had been, she'd missed being able to touch him.

They caught their breath with their limbs tangled together, their bodies moist with perspiration. When Ally was finally able to move, she looked up at the headboard. "I broke it," she said, mortified.

Travis looked up and his face broke into a broad grin. "I'll get you another one. That's good for my ego. I take it that's another first?"

"Definitely," she verified with a sigh. "I guess every woman should get it so good that she breaks a headboard at least once in her life."

Travis kissed her gently on the forehead. "Sweetheart, you can break as many headboards as you want. I wouldn't complain."

And then, to Ally's surprise, he actually laughed, and it was a sound so contagious and rare, that she found herself joining him, both of them whooping until they were breathless all over again.

When they finally made it down to the kitchen, Ally's dinner was pathetic, but Travis swore it was the best meal he ever ate. Ally knew he was lying, but it was the sweetest lie she'd ever heard.

Later that night, Ally was jolted out of an exhausted sleep as she felt Travis suddenly sit up in a motion so swift that it made her whole body shift, her head dropping back on the pillow as it slid off his shoulder. Pushing herself up into a sitting position, she could hear his erratic breathing and there was just enough moonlight to make out his face.

"Travis?" she questioned softly, wanting to know that he was okay. "What happened?" She stroked the damp hair on his forehead, her concern elevating another notch.

He groaned and swiped his palms over his face. "Something's wrong with Kade." Getting out of the bed, he quickly dressed, buttoning his rumpled shirt as he added, "I have to go." He picked his phone out of the pocket of his pants, walking across the room to turn on a small reading light. He clicked a button on his phone, barking out immediately, "What the hell happened?"

Ally knew he was talking to Kade. Glancing at the clock, she noticed it was almost two o'clock in the morning, but Kade had obviously answered almost immediately.

"Why didn't you call me?" Travis asked, running a hand through his already rumpled hair. "I'm on my way." There was a pause as he listened before he added, "It doesn't matter. I'm coming." He clicked the Off button and shoved the phone back in his pocket.

"What happened?" Ally could see Travis's tortured expression now that he'd turned on the lamp, and it tugged at her heart.

"Asha took a fall down the stairs at their house earlier today. Kade said they checked her over and she and the baby are both okay. But they're keeping her overnight for observation." His voice was ragged and broken. "I'm going to be there in case he needs anything."

"I'm going with you." Ally jumped out of the bed, her concern for Travis, Kade, and Asha setting a fire under her ass.

"No. Don't." Travis's expression was implacable. "She's okay. I just need to be there for Kade."

"How did you know?" Ally asked curiously. Travis wanted to be there for Kade, but Ally wanted to be there for Travis. He looked devastated.

"I wish I would have known in time," Travis growled. "It started with my parents..." His voice dropped off, and he hesitated.

Ally came up beside him and put a comforting hand on his arm. "What about your parents?"

Travis eyes grew dark and cold as he said in an icy tone, "I killed them." He shrugged her hand off his arm, picked up his suit jacket and left the bedroom without another word.

Ally stood there for a moment, her entire body trembling. She heard the door downstairs slam as Travis left, and she stood there for a moment in shock as she heard his Ferrari fire up.

Running out of the bedroom and down the stairs, she reached the door and flung it open just in time to see his taillights drive away from her house.

She closed the door and locked it, moving mechanically back up the stairs and crawling between the sheets that still smelled like sex…and Travis.

Her mind whirled over what had just happened, and the pain she'd seen on Travis's face. As pieces of the puzzle fell into place, she buried her face in Travis's pillow and wept.

Ally didn't get much sleep that night, wanting desperately to go to Travis, but knowing he needed time and that the hospital wasn't the place for a confrontation. When she finally got word of Asha the next day, it was from Asha herself. She called Ally, complaining about Kade's behavior, and about the fact that he wanted to move their bedroom downstairs so she didn't have to climb the stairs again. Every time she walked up or down the stairs, Kade was right behind her or in front of her, ready to stop her from falling.

Ally smiled as Asha went on and on, obviously disgruntled. Other than a few body aches, Asha was fine. But Kade was on her ass every minute of the day.

"Kade loves you, and I think you scared him pretty badly. You're pregnant, Asha. Give him time," she told Asha patiently.

"I know." Asha sighed over the phone line. "He'll lighten up eventually when he sees me go up and down the stairs safely enough times."

Ally laughed, knowing Asha adored Kade, and her complaining was more out of concern for Kade than her own inconvenience.

After she hung up with Asha, Ally finished reading one of her books on adult children of alcoholics, incredulous about how she had every one of the negative behaviors that seemed to develop in children growing up with alcoholic parents. She'd been reading everything she could to try to learn more about her behavior and how to break free from her negative self-image.

"And then I went out and picked the worst man I could possibly have chosen for a partner," she mumbled to herself unhappily.

Strangely, she felt like she'd already started breaking some of her bad habits, refusing to believe the negative voices in her head as truth, and she'd work on the rest. Or maybe it wasn't so odd, since she realized that Travis had started the process, had helped her to start deviating from her normal negative thoughts about herself.

Ally wished Travis had called himself, but maybe he was home getting some much-needed sleep, although she doubted it. Most likely he was hiding, running away. It was her last day of vacation. She'd see him at work tomorrow.

With that satisfying thought, she went to her computer to write.

Chapter 13

T ravis had obviously arrived on the upper floor, the usual quiet falling over the employees as he made his way to his office. Ally did her usual countdown:

"Five…

"Four…

"Three…

"Two…

"One…"

Travis strode through the doors exactly on time, but he didn't say a word. He shot a sideways glance at her, scowled and proceeded into his office without saying one damn thing to her.

Somehow, Ally had already expected that reaction. She got to her feet, smoothing down her cream-colored cashmere sweater dress, loving the feel of the material under her fingers. It was perfectly professional, with a decorative belt that clipped at the waist and hung comfortably at her hips. But it was a little bit shorter than her normal style, the hem hitting above the knees, and the material clung to every curve. The matching stilettos were plain but elegant, and she loved the whole outfit. She just tried not to cringe when she imagined what the ensemble had probably cost.

She shook her head as she went to the kitchen and poured a mug of coffee. Travis was never going to let her take back any of the clothes he'd bought, so she might as well wear them.

Not bothering to knock, Ally opened the door of Travis's office, locked it quietly behind her, and placed the mug on his desk. "Your coffee, Mr. Harrison."

His eyes never left the computer screen. "Fine," he grumbled.

She was right. Travis was hiding, and doing a lousy job of it. Their awareness of each other was electric in the air. Time for more drastic measures.

"You left something at my house," she told him in a low, sultry voice.

He looked up then, his eyes turning dark as he saw his black tie dangling from her fingers. Leaning forward, he reached for it with a frown, but Ally held it away. Moving around the desk, she positioned herself behind his chair.

"I don't think so, Travis." She yanked his shoulders against the back of the chair and slipped the tie around him, pinning him and making a tight knot that restricted his body at the elbows.

He could have easily fought her, but he just sat there dumbfounded as she moved around in front of him and purred, "I think since I gave you your appetizer, you can repay me by giving me breakfast." She leaned down before he could say a word, speared her fingers through his hair and kissed him, an embrace that meant business. He responded immediately, his tongue dueling with hers as she kissed him deeply, languorously, removing her hands from his hair and started to unbutton his pristine shirt, jerking it out of his waistband and opening every button she could get to as she nipped at his lips and soothed them with her tongue. When she loosened the buttons on all but the top few that were restricted by his tie, she took her mouth from his and straightened. Placing one stiletto-clad foot on the leather chair right between his legs, she gave his chair a hard shove, and it rolled back just enough to allow her to sink to her knees.

One thing that had always bothered her was the fact that Travis never let her touch him this way, too worried about losing control before he satisfied her. Didn't he know that she needed to touch him just as much as he wanted to touch her?

"Ally, what the fuck are you doing?" Travis's voice was hoarse and deeply aroused.

"I'm...exploring," she told him, giving his own words back to him. "I want to know what you like. Tell me what you like." She parted the material of his shirt and traced her tongue over the majestic phoenix on his chest. He'd told her why and how he'd gotten it, that it symbolized his dedication to weather the storm of the controversy after the death of his parents. "You're so strong, Travis."

She bit one of his nipples and then soothed it with her tongue. His body tensed, but he didn't move, didn't fight. She repeated the action on the other one, and then trailed her tongue down his ripped abdomen, moaning at the feel of his skin as her fingers trailed down the same path. Her nimble fingers undid his belt, flipped open the button of his pants and lowered the zipper. She yanked on his black boxer briefs, liberating his cock, which almost looked like it was twitching anxiously and fully erect. She wrapped her fingers around the engorged member and sighed as she looked at him, his head tipped back, the corded muscles in his neck straining. "God, you're the hottest man I've ever seen. And you're mine, Travis." She squeezed his cock lightly. "This is mine." She'd already figured out that he liked her claiming him.

"Jesus, Ally. If you don't stop touching me, I'll explode," Travis rasped, his head snapping up to look down at her.

Their eyes met in clash of wills, but Ally was determined to win this time. "That's the whole idea, big guy." She licked her lips hungrily. "I want my breakfast. And I want to taste you until you lose your mind."

"Already there," he answered darkly.

"Not yet. But you will be. I've wanted this since the first time you kissed me. It's one of my fantasies. And I'm in charge right now." She knew she really wasn't, that he was letting her do this, but it didn't matter.

"My fantasy, too," Travis growled.

Ally wanted to ask him why he'd never let her do it, but she already knew the answer. Travis was totally unselfish when it came to giving her pleasure. What he didn't realize was that it pleased her to give him that same ecstasy.

Lowering her mouth to him, Ally twirled her tongue over the sensitive head of his cock, lapping up a drop of salty moisture dotting the tip, sucking it off leisurely.

"You're going to kill me," Travis groaned, threading his hands through her hair, causing her hair clip to drop to the floor.

She let the tip of his cock pop out of her mouth. "Do you like that?" she asked innocently, mimicking what he'd done to her just a few nights ago.

"Fuck, yeah. I just don't understand any of this," he panted.

"You don't need to. Just…feel." Ally wrapped her lips around his cock and took him deeply into her mouth, letting her throat relax. Travis was built big, but she took him as far as she possibly could, tightening her lips around the shaft as she let him slide in and out.

"Christ. I'm dying," Travis grunted as he fisted her hair, his hips pumping.

Ally savored every groan that came out of Travis's mouth as she gently fingered his balls, trying to take his cock even deeper into her mouth. She slowly increased her speed, Travis becoming more demanding as his hips jerked up to meet her mouth.

Ally didn't stop as she tilted her eyes up, watching Travis as he watched her, as though riveted to the sight of her sucking him off.

"Fuck. Fuck. Fuck. I'm gonna come, Ally," Travis told her in a guttural tone.

And he did, his cock spilling his warm release into the back of her throat as his body bucked and he groaned her name over and over. Ally kept her mouth on him, savoring every drop of his pleasure, her tongue toying with the head of his cock until he slumped in the chair, obviously sated.

She gently tucked him back into his briefs and put his clothing back together. His eyes were still closed when she moved to the back of the chair and released the knot on the tie.

"Why?" Travis asked in a confused voice.

"Because I wanted to," she replied sweetly. She bent and picked up her hair clip from the floor.

"Jesus. What are you wearing?" Travis exploded.

Ally smiled at him. "One of the dresses you bought me. I didn't have any matching lingerie, so I bought my own." She knew he'd seen the sexy panties and the top of her garters. She'd done it on purpose. Lifting the hem of the dress, she gave him a peek at the white ensemble underneath. "Isn't it sweet?" It was fairly modest, white with little pink bows.

Travis gaped at her as she let the hem float back down and arranged her hair again in a small decorative mirror on the wall.

Sashaying to the door, she tossed the tie across the room and Travis's quick reflexes caught it in mid-air.

"For the next time I'm naughty." She unlocked and opened the door, looking back at him as she swung it open. "Enjoy your coffee, Mr. Harrison. But just for the record, I'm still not getting your coffee every day. Today was special."

She walked out of the office, closing the door quietly behind her. Her heart was still hammering, her knees weak, knowing what she'd just done had been a risk. But she'd already decided that a life without some risk wasn't worth living. With risk came hope. And she'd keep her hopes alive for Travis until all her belief in him was gone, until there was no chance for them. He was worth it. He'd lived in darkness for way too long, and he needed to conquer his demons or let them destroy his life. He'd been there when she needed someone to believe in her, and she wanted to do the same for him. Because, truth was, she trusted him more than any other person on earth. Now he just needed to trust himself.

Ally went to the restroom and cleaned herself up before returning to her desk.

She stared at Travis's office door for a long time before going back to work.

Travis sat totally immobile for a long time, stunned as he looked at the door where Ally had exited.

His coffee was tepid, but he gulped it down anyway, trying to figure out if what had happened was really truth or if it was just a very vivid fantasy he'd conjured up because of his need for Ally.

Why isn't she running?

His first shock had come when he discovered that Ally was actually at her desk today. He hadn't expected her to be. Not after what he'd said the night he'd left her to go to the hospital. Had she been so tired she hadn't really gotten what he'd told her?

He could have easily stopped what had happened this morning, but he hadn't wanted to, hadn't even been able to wrap his mind around the fact that he hadn't been experiencing some sort of surreal fantasy. He fingered the tie on his desk, proof that she'd really been here. Part of him wanted to just go on and see what happened now, not confront any reality. Hell...reality sucked. He'd much rather preserve the dream. But his relationship with Ally was never going to progress until he faced her down, figured out what was going on in that complicated brain of hers.

He pushed the intercom button. "Alison, I need you." As he let off the button, he admitted to himself that truer words had never been spoken.

He waited as she let herself into the office, his cock hardening as he viewed the innocent-looking dress that was, in reality, a cock torture device. It hugged her body in all the right places, and dammit...it was way too short. Had that really been one of the outfits he'd purchased for her? He hated it. No...he actually loved it, but he didn't want another man seeing her shapely body in the garment. And he sure as hell didn't want anybody else to see what she was wearing underneath. It was white, for Christ's sake. But Travis had just decided that white underwear with cute pink bows was the hottest thing he'd ever seen. Maybe it was speaking to his caveman: the virginal, sweet color making him want to drag Ally off and corrupt her as soon as possible.

Ally seated herself in front of his desk, a cup of coffee in her hand. She'd fixed her hair, and she looked every inch a prim, composed assistant. Hell...even *that* made him crazy.

"You wanted me, Mr. Harrison?" she asked politely.

Yeah. He wanted her all right. But nobody would ever know that the woman sitting in front of him had a few minutes ago been a sexual goddess on her knees, sucking his cock until his head had nearly blown off. He cleared his throat and asked, "What just happened here this morning, Alison?"

"Did I ever tell you that I hate the name Alison? My mother used to call me that, and I don't like being called by that name, which is why I prefer people to call me Ally," she answered in a calm, informative voice. "And as far as what happened? I believe that you stomped into the office without saying a word. I then brought you your coffee...which I almost never do. Then I tied my obstinate billionaire boss from Hell to his chair and proceeded to give him a blow job until he had an orgasm. I think I did something I've wanted to do for a very long time, making my fantasies of touching you any way I wanted come true. Does that sound correct?" she asked him pertly. "Oh, then I gave him back the tie that he left at my house after using it to give me multiple orgasms," she added casually and took a sip from her mug, raising a questioning brow at him.

Travis nearly choked on the last of his coffee. "What the hell has gotten into you?" Travis asked, squirming in his chair from hearing Ally bluntly recounting the morning.

"Nothing got into me. I gave you a blow job, but you never really got into me."

Holy Christ! She was trying to make him crazy. He knew she was. "I'll never call you by your full name again if you hate it. You should have told me." He paused before asking, "Do you remember what I told you when I left to help Kade? Did you hear what I said?"

"I heard you," she affirmed.

"Why are you still here?"

"Why wouldn't I be? I work here." She sat her coffee on the desk and put her hands on the surface of the wood, giving him a stubborn glare. "I assume that what you meant that night is that you had a precognitive dream about your parents, and you ignored it, thinking it was just a nightmare. Therefore, you blame yourself because you didn't stop what happened. You did not kill your parents, Travis. Your father killed your mother and then himself. He was mentally ill. It's time for you to stop torturing yourself because you didn't know the dream would really come true. It was not your fault."

Travis gaped at Ally, her fierceness stunning him. Her gaze was wild and ferocious, and protective as hell. And all that strong protectiveness was centered on him. "It was the first time it happened," he admitted. "I hate myself for not saving my mother. If I had just paid attention—"

"You. Didn't. Know." Ally emphasized every word. "What else happened after that?"

Travis looked at her, surprised. "It doesn't happen very often. And sometimes I still don't believe it, but I act on it if I dream of someone dying or getting hurt. Precognition isn't accepted in mainstream science. It isn't supposed to happen. There's no proof that it even exists."

"And there's no proof that it doesn't," Ally shot back at him.

"You believe in it?"

Ally sat slowly back down in her chair. "You told me once that I was pragmatic on the surface and a dreamer inside. I write fantasy because I believe anything is possible, that there are still so many things in this world that we can't explain. So I try very hard not to discount anything. I don't *not* believe in a lot of things. Things like precognition can't be proved or disproved." She sighed and gave him an earnest look. "But I can tell you that I absolutely believe in you. Tell me about it, Travis. Please."

Ally's understanding, compassionate look broke Travis. He buried his face in his hands and spoke. "Like I said, it really doesn't happen that often. You're right about what happened with my parents. Looking back, it's hard not to regret that I didn't pay attention, but I thought it was just a nightmare. Then I started having recurring dreams about Mia. The first time, I dreamed that she was being abused. She was still in school, and I flew there just to reassure myself that she was okay. But the dreams were correct. She was with an abusive boyfriend, the same asshole who tried to hurt her once he got out of prison after I put him there for abusing her. She was married to Max when he got out of prison and came after her the second time, and I had a dream that she was running away, Max and Kade found her, and her ex killed all of them."

"So that's why you hid her, why you didn't tell Kade and Max? And you saved her from the abusive boyfriend when she was in school. Your dreams actually saved her twice," Ally said breathlessly. "That's incredible."

"I never knew Kade's accident was going to happen. I wish to hell I had known. But the night I woke you up, I'd just had a dream that he was in a hospital waiting room, distraught. I knew something was wrong, but I didn't know what had happened. Unfortunately, it wasn't a warning. The dreams just happen, and sometimes not nearly soon enough to prevent anything. And I had a vague dream about Asha that her ex-husband tried to kill her. That's why I asked Tate to stay near her while his broken leg was healing. I had the same vague dream again the night before she was attacked by her ex-husband."

"And Tate saved her life," Ally finished, having already heard that story from Asha.

"Yes," Travis admitted.

"So your family knows?"

"No," Travis replied irritably. "What am I going to tell them, Ally? They'll think I'm as crazy as my father."

"No, they will not," Ally answered, her voice infuriated. "They'd never think that. Travis, you have a gift, a gift that saved both Mia's life and Asha's. It's nothing to be ashamed about."

He looked up at her dubiously. "My father was certifiable, Ally. And it isn't a gift. I think it's a goddamn curse. It's not predictable. It doesn't always help—"

"It has helped. I understand your frustration over not having control over it. But it saved your sister and your sister-in-law. "

"It makes me different. Separate from everyone else. I've always hated it," Travis growled. "But yeah, since it helped Mia and Asha, I'd rather have it and be different than to see either of them harmed."

"It makes you special. And you allow it to separate you. Especially from your family," Ally argued. "I'm not saying you have to tell the whole world, but the people who care about you will understand. I think they'd accept it better than you think."

Would they really? Travis thought about what he imagined Ally's reaction would be to him, and he'd been totally wrong. Was it possible that he was so afraid that people would think he was as crazy as his father that he was overreacting? "I'll think about it," he grumbled.

"Thank you," Ally said, her face lighting up in a smile.

Travis felt like he'd just gotten sucker punched in the gut. He wanted to tell Ally how much it meant to him that she could accept him as he was, but he didn't know how. "I'm glad you didn't leave me," he told her in a husky voice. Not exactly what he'd wanted to say, but he meant those words too. Really, he was more than glad. His whole world had crumbled when he thought he'd never see her again, that he'd never see her sweet smile directed at him in the future. Her take-charge attitude and naughty words this morning had nearly made him come unglued, and she was actually becoming a cock teaser, which he loved. As long as the only cock she teased was his. Ally was starting to recognize her own sexuality, and he found that budding boldness erotic as hell. The fact that she hadn't rebuffed him because of his peculiar ability of precognition, and had in fact accepted it quite easily, had sealed her fate. She was his forever. She just hadn't entirely realized it yet.

"You're worth fighting for, Travis, even if it did test my boundaries a little."

He hated the vulnerability in her voice. "Baby, there are no boundaries between us. You can cross any lines with me at any time. Especially like you did this morning," he rasped, trying not to remember watching her go down on him with such rampant enthusiasm.

"I want you to trust me," she said, slightly forlorn.

"I do. It's me I didn't trust. Forgive me?"

Travis watched as she pretended to contemplate his words for a minute, a period of time when he didn't even breathe.

"Mmmm…I suppose. But it might take a little making up on your part." She gave him a sultry smile.

"Name it," he agreed eagerly, finally taking a breath. There was nothing he wasn't prepared to give Ally.

She pulled a bound manuscript from its place beside her from her chair. "Read the next book and give me your honest opinion. I had time to finish it while I was on vacation."

Travis hadn't even noticed that she'd brought it into the office with her, probably because he'd been too busy noticing her cock torture device of a dress. He snatched it eagerly, excited that she'd finished the next book. "That's not a make-up, sweetheart. That would be my pleasure."

"Then can I have one more thing?" she asked hesitantly.

"Tell me."

"Will you let me touch you like I did this morning more from now on?"

Travis nearly groaned aloud. Ally would kill him, but in a good way. He was giving her anything she wanted, and her only request was to be able to touch him more? He was a damn billionaire, capable of making her every dream come true, yet all she seemed to want was…him. "If you do it, you'd better be ready for a quickie," he warned her dangerously.

"No problem," she told him with a wicked smile. "You recover very quickly."

Now *that* was the truth when it came to Ally. He had another erection within five minutes of fucking her. "I'll try," he grumbled.

Her face lit up so joyously that Travis decided he'd let her do any damn thing she wanted to do to him, as long as she looked at him exactly that way for the rest of his life. She might be the death of him, but he'd die a very happy man.

Chapter 14

Their trip to Colorado the next day was uneventful, but for Ally, it was spectacular. She'd never been in Travis's private jet, and the luxury of the aircraft was unbelievable to her. Of course Travis had wanted to spend most of their flight time showing her the bedroom, which she gladly enjoyed right along with him.

She leaned back in the leather seat of the BMW she'd rented for him, unable to find him the Ferrari he'd requested. "Sorry you have to slum it with the BMW," she told him facetiously.

"I guess I'll just have to be a regular guy," he answered with a grin.

She snickered, knowing Travis Harrison would never be just a regular man. "Yeah, just a real average Joe," she agreed, nodding her head. "With two security vehicles following us from the minute we left that luxury jet."

"Tate's guys," Travis said, disgruntled, maneuvering through traffic once they left the city limits of Denver. "You'll be pretty safe once we get to Rocky Springs."

"Me? It's not me they're protecting, Travis."

"Of course it is. That's the only reason I told Tate to send more than one. I wanted to be alone on the flight, so I left your security at the airport back in Florida, and told Tate to send some of his guys to the airport here. I don't worry much about my own security. I worry about yours."

"I've never had security before." She looked at him, puzzled.

"Sweetheart, your beautiful ass has been tailed ever since your ex showed up at your house. You just didn't know it."

"Why?"

"Because you're my woman and whether I like it or not, I'm a high-profile man. I want to make sure you're safe." He shot her a look not to argue with him.

"I didn't know," she murmured, not sure how she felt about being watched all the time, but touched that he was thinking about her safety. "I'm sure it's not necessary."

"It is," Travis replied harshly. "Don't argue with me on this one, Ally. I want you safe."

Deciding she could deal with security because it was just part of who Travis was, she replied, "Okay." She watched the scenery out the window, marveling at the high peaks of the mountains, the top of which still had snow. "Oh my God. Are those bighorn sheep?" she asked excitedly, looking at the rocky terrain by the side of the freeway.

"Yep," Travis replied. "You've never seen one?"

"Never," Ally replied enthusiastically. "I've rarely gotten out of Florida." She rummaged in her purse for her phone to take a picture.

"Don't bother," Travis advised. "You're too far away. Don't worry. You'll see plenty of wildlife here."

"You know, that's one of the things I was really excited about when I took this job. I wanted to travel, see other places. I was disappointed once I realized you'd never take me. But I guess it all worked out because I needed my other job." She put her phone back in her purse.

"I wanted to," Travis answered hoarsely. "But I couldn't, Ally. It wasn't possible. Even then, I wanted to fuck you. And to have you that close to me would have killed me."

"It's so hard to believe you were really attracted to me for that long. Travis, there are so many women who—"

"Didn't matter. I haven't fucked another woman since I met you. I didn't want a single one of them," he said irritably.

Ally gaped at him. "You haven't had sex in four years?"

"Nope. Just me and my fantasies about doing the only woman I wanted. But they were pretty hot fantasies," he said jokingly, trying to lighten the conversation.

"Why didn't I ever notice?" Ally muttered to herself.

"Because I didn't want you to. You were engaged to another man. I thought you actually had the perfect life. But if I had known he was a dick, that he wasn't making you happy, I would have started taking you with me," he answered angrily. "I would have done everything in my power to get you away from him."

Ally felt tears well up in her eyes, the knowledge that Travis had been there all that time wanting her nearly breaking her. She knew how she felt about him now, and if he'd felt even a small portion of what she felt for him, it had to have been difficult. "I wasn't happy. Rick and I hadn't even tried to have sex in two years. He made excuses, but I knew—"

"Don't, Ally. Don't think about him," Travis barked.

"I don't hear his voice anymore, Travis. And I'm actually grateful he made me leave him. It doesn't hurt anymore," she told him honestly.

"Whose voice do you hear?" he asked in a voice cracking with emotion.

"Mine." Ally looked at his profile, his jaw clenched tightly. He obviously still couldn't stand to think about her ex. "And sometimes I hear yours. Especially the naughty things." She watched as he relaxed in his seat, his face softening.

"I wanted to kill the bastard for what he'd done. He's lucky he just lost his job and his woman—if you can even call her that. Christ! She was barely eighteen," Travis grumbled.

"How do you know that?" Ally inquired, slightly stunned that Travis knew about the other woman in Rick's life.

"Because I filtered the right information to the head of his practice to get him fired, and then I bribed the woman to leave him. She was young, and dazzled by the fact that an educated man was interested in her. He'd fed her some line of bullshit about you, and she believed it because she was young and clueless. She never really knew the truth about you. She was mortified, Ally. I didn't want her to destroy her life with an asshole. She was too damn young. I paid her tuition to go to college, provided she stayed away from him. She took the deal, and she told me she'd never see him again anyway."

Ally stared at Travis for a moment, completely blown away. It was hard for her to feel sorry for Rick since she'd worked her ass off for years for him. And he'd get another job. Just not one as prestigious as the one he'd landed after college. But the fact that Travis had saved a young woman from Rick's manipulative behavior touched her. "I knew she was young, but not that young. Thank you. He would have destroyed her." Rick had nearly destroyed her, and she was older and wiser. She could imagine what damage he could do to a woman that young and naïve.

"You're not pissed off?"

"No. Rick will get another job, but he might have to work a little harder. I can't be sad about that. Maybe he'll be too busy to go after barely legal women. But what you did for that girl is amazing. You're amazing," she breathed softly, knowing this wasn't the first young woman he'd rescued. He'd also helped two young Indian women escape a bad fate when he'd been helping Asha.

Travis shrugged, looking almost embarrassed. "I thought it was the right thing to do."

"It was," Ally agreed, her chest tightening when she looked at Travis. He had so much integrity, so much hidden compassion inside him. And he never sought anything in return, never wanted recognition for the good things he did. In fact, he avoided the attention. Travis Harrison did what he thought was right, because of his sense of honor. "You're one hell of a man, Travis Harrison."

"I'm an asshole, Ally. And everyone knows it. But if you think that, I'm glad you're delusional," he said with a smirk. "Whatever it takes to keep you," he added in a more serious tone.

Ally rolled her eyes. "And you think I'm delusional?" But her whole body flushed with pleasure. "Oh look! We're coming up on the Eisenhower Tunnel," she exclaimed, seeing the sign that they were getting close.

Travis shook his head, and smiled. "I didn't realize you'd get excited over a big hole in a mountain."

Ally gave him an admonishing look. "You're cynical because you've traveled all over the world. The tunnel is incredible. It will take us right underneath the Continental Divide. And it tops out at over eleven thousand feet high. It's one of the highest and longest vehicular tunnels in the world, Travis."

"You did your research."

"Of course I did. And it wasn't research. It was fun. I've never been to Colorado. It's beautiful here."

"You might not think so when the snow starts to fly," Travis answered wryly.

"I've never seen snow," Ally answered wistfully.

"You will. You'll be going everywhere with me from now on." His statement sounded almost like a warning.

Ally thrilled at Travis's possessive tone of voice as they entered the Eisenhower Tunnel. "This is incredible. We're actually going right through a mountain," she mused, thinking about how surreal it seemed to be in another part of the country, an area so different from Florida. "What's it like in Rocky Springs? How big is the ranch?"

She'd only met Tate Colter a few times in passing, occasions where he stopped into the office to see Travis. He was blond, big, and gorgeous. But the only thing she'd really remembered was his incredible gray eyes and how polite he'd always been to her.

"Ranches," Travis corrected her. "The town is small, but the Colters own over a thousand acres right outside of the town. They all have a ranch there. And then there's a guest ranch, a spa, and ski resort. They have hot springs that run through the area."

"Exactly how many Colters are there?" Ally had never known Tate even had siblings.

"Tate's father is dead. But his mom still lives in the old homestead ranch near the resort with his sister. And he has three other brothers."

"All wealthy, I'm guessing," Ally mused.

"The Colters have been wealthy for generations. Their ancestors settled the town during the gold rush, and they were all innovative and started up some very prosperous ventures. So yeah, they're all obscenely rich." He hesitated for a moment before adding, "But they're great people, too."

Ally was nervous. This wasn't a world she even came into contact with outside of Travis's office. "I hope they like me," she said tentatively. "But at least they think I'm just your assistant."

"That's not what I told Tate. And you're not just my assistant," Travis answered irritably as he exited the freeway and started navigating through a quaint mountain town.

"Then what did you say? We're just…dating."

"I told him I'm bringing my woman," he answered matter-of-factly. "He put us up in one of the guesthouses on his property so we could have privacy. I think Sutherland is taking the other one."

Ally hadn't realized Jason was attending, but she was more concerned about what Travis had told his friends. "But I'm not really your woman. Not really."

"If you say that one more time, I'll pull this vehicle off the road and show you just how much you belong to me," Travis said dangerously, leaving the small town and staying on a two-lane highway, navigating the twists and turns like they were nothing. "Don't say it, Ally. That isn't an empty threat. I'm more than ready to show you exactly what I mean right here and right now."

Oh, God. Ally had never wanted to call him on a threat this badly. Her body ached for him, and she wanted him inside her so desperately that her panties were drenched. But it wasn't exactly a safe area for him to be pulling off the road. And she had no doubt he'd do it. "Show me later," she told him breathlessly.

"Count on it," he warned darkly.

Ally was speechless, thoughts of what exactly Travis would do to her later drifting through her mind. She leaned her head back and closed her eyes, visualizing Travis's powerful body over hers, his fierce look of longing that he always had in his eyes whenever he was inside her.

"What are you thinking about?" Travis asked curiously.

"Nothing," she squeaked guiltily. "Just plotting my third book." *Liar. Liar. I'm so not thinking about a young adult plot at the moment.*

"When is it going to be done? You left me hanging again," he grumbled.

Her eyes shot open. "You already read the second book?"

"Yesterday. And it was fantastic, but you need to end this with a trilogy or you'll drive me crazy."

"I plan on it. And I think you're biased. The publishers hated it," she answered with a sigh, but pleased that Travis seemed to genuinely like the story.

"I don't give a shit what they said. It's fantastic," he grunted. "I'm a reader. So my opinion is much more important," he said arrogantly. "You need a good agent who can submit to the bigger publishing houses. Or you can publish them yourself. I know a good business-man who'd be more than happy to help."

Ally already knew who that good businessman was, and she smiled. "So you'd let Kade help me?"

She laughed when she heard the predictably unhappy growl from Travis that she'd expected. When she stopped laughing, she told him more seriously, "Just the fact that you believe in me is enough. I think this is something I need to accomplish on my own."

"Stubborn woman," he complained mournfully. He nodded his head to the right. "There's a herd of elk."

Ally marveled over the field littered with elk. "They're huge." A few were right beside the road, and Travis slowed down through the area to avoid hitting any of the animals.

After they passed the herd, Ally asked Travis curiously, "So why were you so insistent that I was coming with you to Colorado? You're obviously comfortable with the crowd here. You know the Colters well. Why is this any different than any other charity function?" She'd been wondering that for a while now.

"It's an auction and a ball," Travis answered grimly.

"So? You attend auctions," she shot back at him.

"It's not a typical auction. Tate thought it would be interesting to have a billionaire auction to raise more money. Bastard! And he has the connections to gather a very wealthy crowd."

"So only billionaires will be there?" Ally asked, bewildered.

"No. Billionaires *are* the auction items. Women are bidding on the billionaire of their choice to be their escort for the ball." Travis visibly shuddered. "I can't believe Sutherland showed up. Poor bastard. I hope he knows what he's getting himself into. Tate's own brothers conveniently had to be out of town."

"So you're going to be auctioned off?"

"Hell, no. I'm exempt because I have a woman. It's just the single guys."

"So you brought me along as your cover?" Ally asked, biting back a laugh, knowing that was probably initially the reason he'd needed her.

He hesitated for a moment and then answered, "Yeah. I'm not going up on some auction block like a damn antique or a prize show horse for sale."

Ally snickered. "Well, you are priceless and a stud. That's hilarious. And I think it's very unique. I think it will be fun. And the men who are participating are good sports. Is Tate going to do it?"

"Yeah. Some unsuspecting woman will have to put up with his ornery ass all night," Travis grumbled. "He got a surprising number of men who volunteered. We should raise a lot of money."

"So I'm going to be in the same place as many of the world's most eligible bachelors?" Ally asked teasingly.

"No. You'll be there with me," Travis told her gravely.

"Jason Sutherland will bring a hefty price. So will Tate. I know women who would give anything to spend an evening with either one of them. And I imagine there will be women there with very deep pocketbooks."

"And are you one of those women who would love to spend an evening with Tate or Jason?" Travis questioned, his voice harsh, but a little vulnerable. He turned off the highway and onto a paved road that had a "Welcome to Rocky Springs Resort" sign beside it.

Ally looked at Travis in surprise. Was he serious? Not another man even existed for her anymore. Jason was certainly handsome, and so was Tate. But there was no other guy in the world like Travis. She found it incredible that he could even ask that question, that he still had any doubts. She panted after him like a woman in a perpetual state of heat. It was amazing that Travis had any insecurities, but apparently…he did.

Just like I do.

"No. I'm not." She reached over and gently stroked his rough jawline. "I'm already living my fantasy with you, and I'm lucky enough that it's been more than just one night." She sighed as she stroked the hair at the nape of his neck. "If anything, I wonder why you want me. You're a brilliant, incredibly handsome man who gives to others without any recognition for doing so. I'm just a regular woman, and I'm nothing special. My butt is too big, I'm much too curvy, and I'm not anything out of the ordinary, yet you still want me. Sometimes I'm afraid I'll wake up and realize everything that's happened with you was just one very long, one very hot wet dream. So no…I don't dream or fantasize about any other man but you."

Travis grabbed her hand and brought it to his lips, kissing her palm reverently. "Jesus, Ally. Sometimes I feel exactly the same way."

Time stopped for just a moment, as though only the two of them existed. Ally's breath seized in her lungs, the beauty of Travis leaving himself wide open to her making her heart flip-flop in her chest. Her connection to him was so strong, so right, that she wanted to cry just from the joy of being with him. "I'll never hurt you again, Travis. Not willingly." She released the tremulous breath she'd been holding. "And I'll do whatever it takes to convince you of that. Even if I have to get out your 'naughty boy tie' and tie you up and ravish you until you're completely convinced."

Travis grinned at her wickedly. "I'm suddenly feeling incredibly insecure."

She shot him an equally naughty grin. "Then I guess we'll just have to work on that."

Travis pulled into the driveway of an enormous, beautiful mansion with a circular driveway as he replied, "I'm going to take a lot of damn work."

Even though Ally had butterflies in her belly at the prospect of meeting so many of Travis's peers, she smiled.

Chapter 15

"I think you'll be comfortable here. Travis has stayed here before, so he knows where everything is. Make sure you stay well hydrated and take it easy tonight. We're a little over eight thousand feet here, and you're a flatlander. You might feel the effects of the altitude for a while," Tate told Ally with a charismatic smile. "I'm glad you're here, Ally. I hope you have a good time."

Tate Colter was probably what Travis would call his best friend aside from his brother Kade, but he still wanted to punch him every time he turned that admiring smile toward Ally. "We're fine. You can leave now," Travis told him gruffly, looking around the guesthouse. He had stayed here many times before, and it was a nice place. But all he wanted was for Tate's ass to leave. A ranch hand had brought their bags over earlier, while they'd sat and chatted with Tate over dinner. Now all Travis wanted was to be alone with Ally.

"Glad to know you missed me so much, buddy." Tate slapped Travis on the back with a smirk.

Travis glared back at him, knowing Tate was just trying to push his buttons. It hadn't taken long for Tate to realize that Travis was feeling territorial about Ally, and he'd immediately started paying as much attention to her as possible just to irritate Travis. Bastard!

Ally stepped forward and offered Tate her hand. "Thank you so much for having me. It's beautiful here."

"I'm very happy to have you," Tate answered, putting his emphasis on the word "have" intentionally as he shook Ally's hand much longer than he needed to.

"If you don't leave, I'm gonna fucking kill you," Travis growled.

Tate let go of Ally's hand and let out a choked laugh. "Okay, okay. I'm going." Tate obviously noted that Travis was getting close to his tipping point.

Travis gave him a hard shove, moving Tate closer to the door, not an easy feat since he and Tate were about the same size. But Travis had irritation on his side. Opening the door, he motioned Tate impatiently through the entrance, and slammed it behind him, flipping the lock noisily. He could hear Tate's booming laughter as he walked away from the guesthouse. "Son of a bitch!"

"Travis. He was just giving you a hard time. He isn't interested in me," Ally said soothingly behind him. "Show me the house. It's gorgeous."

"I know what he was trying to do. I swear I'll repay the favor someday." He couldn't wait until Tate had a serious love interest now.

The guesthouse was an expansive ranch, all on one floor. He took Ally by the hand and led her around the various rooms, stopping when he finally reached the master bedroom and slid open the sliding door to the patio off the bedroom. "My favorite part of this house."

Ally stepped outside and sighed, a sound that had Travis's hard cock twitching, wanting to hear that sound as he buried himself inside her.

"It's lovely. And the skies are so clear here. The stars look incredible," she said with awe. "What is this?" She waved toward a small pool with a waterfall that trickled down several ledges of rocks.

"It's the hot springs. They have an incredible flow on this land that allows them to divert it to several places. The biggest one is in the resort and spa."

Ally sniffed loudly. "It has a different smell."

"It's the minerals. This is a natural hot springs. It has like fourteen or fifteen different natural minerals."

"It's beautiful. Is it warm?"

"It is," Travis said casually as he grabbed the hem of his shirt and pulled it over his head. "And relaxing."

Travis nearly groaned as he saw the look of longing on Ally's face as her eyes roamed over his chest. "I'll go get us some water. Tate is right. You need to keep drinking water."

"I'll get it," she answered quickly, licking her lips as she watched him flip the top button of his jeans. She backed up slowly and headed for the kitchen, as though she didn't want to take her eyes away from him.

Travis quickly stripped off his jeans and briefs and slid into the pool, groaning as the warm mineral water sloshed over his body. He submerged himself, letting the warmth soothe him as he dunked his head and then sat on one of the lower rock ledges, leaning back so the water trickled over him, relaxing his muscles.

How often had he sat in this exact place, dreaming about Ally? He'd left the patio light off, leaving only the light from the bedroom on. He looked up at the sky, marveling at the miracle that she was finally here with him. Unconsciously, he gripped his hard, pulsating cock, stroking it as he stared up at the sky, both exhilarated and terrified at how Ally had changed his life. Let's face it, he wasn't a guy who'd had a whole lot of happiness in his life, and it was intoxicating. But he still had fears of losing Ally. And he knew that now he'd never survive the loss.

A small, needy moan came from beside the pool, and Travis looked up to see Ally with two giant bottled waters in her hand, looking at him with so much longing that his heart accelerated like a race car taking off from the starting line. Finally realizing that he was stroking his own cock, he froze.

"Don't stop," Ally begged him quietly. "Please. You look so hot." She set the waters down next to the pool and pulled her delicate short-sleeved shirt over her head in a slow, seductive move.

At that moment, Travis couldn't have stopped if he wanted to. He watched as she slowly stripped for him, her bra coming off next in languid, sensual motions of Ally's upper body. Travis's hand moved up and down his shaft, gripping himself tightly as he watched her, knowing her every movement was meant to arouse him, and it did. Painfully. Her unabashedly sensual movements drove him mad. "God, you're beautiful," he told her hoarsely, their gazes locked on each other.

She cupped her breasts, running her thumbs over the nipples, gasping as she watched him jerking his hand up and down his cock. "God, yes. Touch yourself, Ally." Watching her pleasure her own body nearly broke him.

He saw her bite her bottom lip, trying to hold back her moans of pleasure. She was standing directly in front of the light coming from the bedroom, and she looked like a fucking goddess.

She moved her hands and slowly undid the button and the zipper of her jeans, shimmying out of them, revealing her body slowly, taking her panties with them. Finally, she stood in front of him boldly and beautifully naked, no longer shy about revealing herself to him completely.

"Come to me," Travis ordered, unable to stand another second without touching her.

She slid into the pool silently, the water rippling over her breasts. Placing her hands on his thighs as she arrived in front of him, she slid her hands up and down the muscles, massaging him.

Travis moved his hand from his cock and reached out for her. "Come ride me, Ally. Convince me that you're really here with me," he told her in a pleading but commanding voice.

For once, he wasn't going to hurry this moment. It was too magical, and he wanted to savor Ally the way he'd always needed to, but had never been able to accomplish.

"I almost just wanted to watch you come. You looked so amazing," she told him breathlessly.

Travis's heart skipped a beat, his arousal growing even hotter. What woman said something like that? Only Ally. And it made him want to please her even more. "You're coming with me, baby," he told her adamantly as he lifted her onto the ledge and into his lap. She straddled him, and he reveled in the slick heat of her pussy as she nudged her hips into his groin. Locking his arms around her waist, he put his lips to her neck, nipping and stroking her skin with his tongue. He took his time, relishing every touch, feeling her body quiver in his arms as he latched onto one of her nipples and then giving the other one the same attention. Lifting his head, he demanded, "Kiss me." He put a hand behind her neck and guided her mouth to his.

He explored her mouth with his tongue slowly, loving the way she followed his lead, entangling her tongue with his, bringing them closer than they'd ever been before. Moving his hand down to his cock, he groaned into her mouth when he parted her folds and his fingers found nothing but hot, wet need between her thighs. He guided his cock to her tight channel, pressing his hips up to enter her. She moved then, bearing down on his cock until he was completely buried inside her.

She moaned into his embrace and threaded her hands through his hair, neither of them moving for a moment. Travis luxuriated in the feel of her lips on his, her inner muscles gloving his cock with warmth. Hot mineral water flowed over them as they lost themselves to sensation.

Ally rotated her hips slowly as she fisted his hair, breaking off their kiss to pant beside his ear. Travis grasped her hips, thrusting upward, wanting to fill Ally so completely that she'd crave him forever. In that moment, Travis realized he wasn't just fucking anymore; he was making love with the woman who melded with him so perfectly that he never wanted it to end. Truth was, he'd always been making love with Ally, and it had always been so much more. She was fucking perfection. "Make love to me, Ally. I can't believe you're really here."

"Yes," she moaned as she rotated her hips faster. "I've always been making love to you. And I never want to stop."

Travis pulled her body against his, felt her heart hammering in the same rhythm as his, their bodies both jolting every time they joined together.

They climaxed at the same time, both of them groaning as their lips locked together, Travis feeling her milking his cock as he exploded deep inside her, rocking his world totally and completely.

They stayed locked together, panting as they recovered from the earth-shattering lovemaking they'd just experienced together. Finally, Travis slid down into the water, sitting on the lowest ledge, taking Ally with him to sit between his legs. She rested her head back on his shoulder and he tightened his arms around her waist. "You were meant to be mine, Ally," he whispered into her ear hoarsely.

"I know," she answered simply, gazing up at the sky. "Look, it's a shooting star. Make a wish, Travis."

He'd never been the type of guy to do something as silly as wish upon a star. He was pragmatic, an asshole. He didn't believe any wish on a star would come true. But one wish came immediately to mind:

I wish Ally would fall in love with me and stay with me forever.

Okay...maybe he was a realist, but he could use all the help he could get.

"Did you do it?" she asked excitedly. "I did. But you can't tell. You can only tell me if your wish comes true."

"I did," he confirmed. "Did you?"

"Yes," she answered quietly.

He wondered what she'd wished for, and he fervently hoped that someday he'd be able to tell her that his wish had been granted.

"Hope is getting married." Jason Sutherland downed another slug of his drink, his voice full of despair. "What the hell? She went back to the same asshole she was with in Aspen. I thought I was giving her time to heal, and she went back to the bastard. All he wants is her money. Doesn't she get that? Christ! I should have just pushed her harder after what happened between us at the holidays."

Travis actually felt for the poor guy. He'd walked up to Tate's house after putting Ally to bed because she was tired and had a mild headache, probably the result of the altitude. He'd have to head back soon and check on her. But he and Tate were currently wrapped up in trying to get the distraught Sutherland to calm the hell down.

Tate barely knew Sutherland, but he said sympathetically, "So what are you going to do? If you've been crazy for this woman for years, don't you think it's time to make your move?"

"It's complicated. Her brother Grady is one of the East Coast Sinclairs. And one of my best friends. I've known Hope for years and none of the Sinclair brothers know I want to fuck their sister. Bad," he answered unhappily. "We had one fucking incredible night together at the holidays…and then we had a disagreement. I was going to just bide my time, wait until she was ready. But I'm done waiting. I'm going after her. She's not marrying this asshole."

Tate whistled quietly. "The Sinclairs are a pretty powerful family. You sure you want to tangle with one of their own?"

Jason gave Tate a disgruntled look. "I want to do more than tangle with her."

Travis couldn't help but feel sorry for Sutherland. He'd been in the exact same boat with Ally when she was engaged to another man. "I'm sure your friends would rather see her with you than some guy who just wants to drain her bank account."

"Honestly, it doesn't matter what they think anymore. Hope is the only one who matters," Jason confided angrily.

"You think she's really in love with this guy?" Travis asked curiously, relating Ally's situation to Hope's, and it annoyed the hell out of him. Obviously, some loser was latching onto Hope Sinclair for her money, using her like Ally's ex had used her.

"No. But Hope has a huge heart. She's likely to fall for just about any sad story."

Travis watched a slow smile form on Tate's face, a smile he'd seen before, and it scared the shit out of him. Tate was forming a plan, and it was likely to be trouble.

"I have an idea," Tate confirmed. "But it would be questionably illegal and pretty damn devious. How far are you willing to go to get this woman?"

Jason shrugged. "As far as I need to go. It doesn't matter."

"She could end up hating you," Tate warned.

"Better than her being indifferent and marrying some other guy. Let's hear it."

Travis listened as Tate outlined a plan so outrageous that even he was surprised. The crazy thing was…it just might work. Tate was ex-military Special Forces, and he had balls of titanium sometimes in the crazy shit he was willing to do. But he was also an excellent strategic planner.

"You ready to take that kind of risk?" Tate asked Jason bluntly.

"Yeah. It would give me exactly what I want," Jason answered in a dangerous tone.

That clenched it for Travis. Jason really was in love with this woman. Either that or he was as crazy as Tate.

"I'll help you any way I can." If the guy loved the woman that much, he'd do whatever he could to help Jason. God knew he could sympathize with his situation.

"I will need a favor," Jason answered slowly.

"What is it?"

"I'm going to have to leave in the morning. And I'm scheduled for the auction. I can't leave them hanging now. Can you take my place?"

Travis balked at the thought. "I can't. I'm here with Ally." He wouldn't mind the humiliation to help Sutherland out, but he couldn't do that to Ally, and he didn't want to be with any other woman for an entire night except her.

"I'd be more than happy to entertain Ally for you," Tate said wickedly.

"You'll have your own date. And if you touch her, I'll kill you," Travis grunted, just the thought of leaving Ally unclaimed for the evening making him irritable.

"Just have her bid on you and win," Jason suggested. "I'll cover the tab."

That could work. Travis might have a few moments of humiliation, but Ally would do it. "I'll cover it. I'd pay anything for a night with Ally."

"Thanks. I'll owe you, Travis," Jason told him gratefully.

"No, you won't. Just get the woman and I'll consider us even. No woman deserves to marry someone who's just out to use her," he rumbled, thinking about Ally. He wanted Sutherland to be successful, both for the guy's sake, and Hope Sinclair's.

Travis stood, ready to get back to the guesthouse. "I need to get back and check on Ally."

"I told you to take it easy because of the altitude, Trav. You do something to leave her breathless?" Tate asked in a pseudo innocent voice.

Travis thought about their earth-shattering lovemaking earlier in the hot springs pool. He glared at Tate as he answered, "I sure the hell hope so." Turning to Sutherland, he added, "Good luck. I hope it all works out." He shook Jason's hand and headed for the door, silently hoping that this woman Jason cared about was as smart and had a heart as big as Jason claimed she did. She was definitely going to need it.

Chapter 16

Ally couldn't remember an occasion when she'd been more nervous in her entire life. She smoothed down the silky material of the black cocktail dress, wondering if she should change. It was sexy and dressy, but the hem ended at mid-thigh, and exposed way more of her legs than she usually showed. The black stiletto heels were extremely high, and the neckline plunged down to the valley of her breasts, making it impossible for her to wear a bra with the ensemble. Luckily, the top portion that covered her breasts had heavier material and pleats that covered everything. Still, she felt naked without a bra.

She took one last stare at herself in the mirror, murmuring to herself, "You can do this. They're just people."

But those people would be looking at her because she was bidding for Travis. He'd explained to her this morning about what had happened with Jason Sutherland, and what he needed her to do. She wasn't exactly comfortable bidding with Travis's money, but he'd looked so vulnerable that she would do anything to get him out of an obligation he obviously hated. And it really touched her that he was doing it for Jason.

They'd had a quiet day, Travis hovering over her and plying her with fluids and carbs—just what her hips didn't need—to help her weather the altitude issue. She'd honestly felt just fine since the morning, her reaction obviously mild, and Travis's concern had been way over the top. Strangely, she didn't mind, finding it more sweet than irritating.

"Holy Christ! Please tell me that's not what you're wearing tonight." Travis's growl sounded from the doorway of the bedroom.

Ally looked at the displeasure on Travis's face and her heart plummeted to her feet. "I don't look good in it. I knew I should have picked something else," she told him, disheartened.

"No, sweetheart, you don't look good. You look like every man's fantasy, a sensual goddess. I'm not sure my heart can take it." He walked over to her and turned her to face him by taking her hand. He caressed her palm with his thumb, his eyes roaming over her body and finally stopping at her face. "There won't be a man in the room who won't want to fuck you. I didn't mean to hurt your feelings with that comment, or your confidence. It's my confidence that's in jeopardy. How am I going to keep a horde of horny men away from you?"

Ally rolled her eyes. "It's not that revealing, and the only man who gets horny when looking at me is you," she assured him, quietly pleased that he thought she looked hot. "And you're looking incredibly handsome yourself, Mr. Harrison." And he did. She saw Travis in a suit all the time, but in a tux, he was absolutely devastating. No doubt he'd have women panting all over him. And she'd definitely be one of the many. "How am I going to keep the women away from you?"

"All they have to see is the way I look at you and they'll get the message loud and clear," he answered, kissing the palm of her hand tenderly.

Ally nearly melted to a puddle right there on the bedroom floor. God, this man could make her feel like the most desirable woman on the planet. And she knew his assessment wasn't even close. But it still made her want to howl with happiness.

"I don't like your earrings, though," Travis said thoughtfully.

Ally fingered the small studs in her ears. They were the best pair of studs she had, and as she was putting them on she was wishing she had got a prettier pair. "I'm sorry. I didn't think to pick up—"

"I think these would look better." He reached into his pocket and pulled out a small, velvet box.

"Travis...you didn't." She took the box with a shaky hand, flipping the lid with a gasp. Nestled in the velvet interior were the most exquisite bracelet and earrings she'd ever seen. They were unique and beautiful, and she instantly suspected who had made them. "Mia?"

"Yes. She makes every item unique and I wanted them to be different from what any other woman would be wearing," Travis answered gruffly. "Put them on."

Ally was torn. She didn't want to reject anything Travis gave her, but as she looked over the glittering stones—black opals and diamonds—she knew they were very valuable and rare. She looked at Travis, his eyes filled with anticipation and anxiety, and pulled the jewelry from the box. Did he really think she wouldn't like them? She pulled out the studs and put in the dangling earrings that had two long strands, alternating the black opals and diamonds. Silently, she handed the bracelet to Travis and let him fasten it around her wrist.

"I wanted to get the necklace, too—"

"No," she told him emphatically, fingering the diamond unicorn around her neck. "I haven't taken this off since you gave it to me, and I never will."

"I figured you'd say that," Travis said with a boyish grin.

Ally looked at herself in the mirror, the sophisticated bracelet and earrings setting off the dress perfectly. "I don't know what to say right now, Travis." She was speechless, unable to express herself past the huge lump in her throat. Nobody had ever given her something so beautiful or so thoughtful...except Travis. "They're so beautiful and I'll be so afraid I'll lose them."

Travis shrugged. "Just tell me you like them. And if you lose them, I'll get you some more. It's just jewelry, Ally."

"Anything you give me is special." She turned and stroked his cheek. "And I want to give you something in return. But what do you give a billionaire?"

He took her hand gently and placed it over his bulging cock. "You give me this. And that's pretty special," he told her with a mischievous grin.

She couldn't help herself. She burst out laughing at his unexpected action. "Pervert," she accused him.

"You gave me your writing, Ally. And you gave me your faith. You give me yourself, sweetheart. Next to that, pieces of jewelry mean very little. So take the gifts I desperately want to give you," he said huskily. "I just want to make you happy."

She stood on her tiptoes and kissed him tenderly. "You already do."

"I can see your breasts." He nudged the fabric of the top aside. "Holy shit! Do I have to think about you being almost naked under that dress all night?" He reached down and slowly lifted the hem of the skirt, hissing as he saw the black stockings and skimpy black panties. He groaned and dropped the skirt. "I'll never make it through this night."

"Of course you will," she answered, her body flushed with pleasure.

"Watch how you sit down. And don't let anyone close enough to see down the top of that dress," Travis ordered in a graveled voice.

"Does that include you?" she asked innocently.

"Hell, no," he exploded. "I'll be leering like a horny degenerate every damn chance I get."

Ally chuckled softly and picked up her black clutch bag. "Showtime for you, billionaire bachelor stud."

"You know what to do?" Travis asked for about the one hundredth time that day.

"Yes. That was a very kind thing you did for Jason," she answered as Travis ushered her out the bedroom door and they descended the stairs hand in hand.

"I wish I would have kept my damn mouth shut," he said grumpily.

Ally smiled, knowing he didn't mean a word of what he'd just said. Travis referred to himself as an asshole, and maybe there were many who were afraid of his sometimes icy exterior. But she knew better. Travis Harrison had a huge heart. It was just unfortunate that most people didn't see him the same way she did.

"Bid high and get it over with," he demanded as he closed the outside door and locked it. "And for God's sake, don't get too close to anyone or bend over. I'll have a heart attack."

Ally shivered at the possessive note in his voice, his concern more about somebody seeing her undergarments than the discomfort he was about to experience.

"Would you like me to find a trench coat to wear?" she asked him jokingly.

As he opened the car door for her, his face lit up hopefully. "Would you?"

"I was kidding, Travis," she said as she laughed delightedly.

"Damn!" he exclaimed unhappily. "I wasn't."

Ally snickered as Travis buckled her seat belt and closed the door, striding around to the driver's side and getting in.

"Thank you for the beautiful gift, Travis." She fingered the bracelet in the dim light, still overwhelmed by the things that Travis did for her that just seemed ordinary to him. "Tell me what I can do for you in return."

"I don't want anything," he told her simply as he started the engine. "I just want you. But if you'd let me rip that dress off you and examine your sexy underwear later, I'd be a happy man."

"Done," she agreed readily, her body already heating just from the thought.

"Best gift ever," he answered with so much excitement and enthusiasm that he sounded like a kid at Christmas.

Once they were on the road to the resort, Travis grasped her hand and placed it on his thigh, as though he just needed to feel her touch. Ally let out a happy sigh and relaxed back into the leather seat, thinking that maybe her introduction into Travis's world wouldn't be so very difficult after all.

When the bidding got close to six figures, Ally started having palpitations. Yes…it was Travis's money she was bidding, but he'd already given so much to this charity, and was generously managing it along with Jason Sutherland and Kade.

The ballroom at the resort was magnificent, but everyone was currently crowded around the small stage in the corner, women practically shoving to get closer to the platform. Travis stood up there, looking calm with his hands in the pockets of his pants, but his eyes never left hers. He kept nodding subtly, encouraging her to go on.

Had he known the bidding would get this high? He'd ended up being the first man up, so Ally had no idea what kind of money this event was going to raise, or how much each "date" was going to bring in.

Bid high and get it over with.

That's what Travis had asked her to do. But how high was high?

Women were bidding furiously, one right after the other, Ally raising her paddle every time the bidding slowed and the auctioneer was waiting for a higher bid. She looked briefly at the women, every one of them dripping with gems, looking like they belonged there.

Travis shot her a slightly uncomfortable and irritated look, telling her he wanted to get the hell off that stage quickly.

Come on, Ally. It's not like Travis can't afford it. Don't think about it. Just rescue him.

"Two hundred thousand," she called out confidently, raising the bet over what she thought most women would bid.

All eyes were on her, most of the women giving her a disgusted look, but Travis just smirked slightly and his eyes danced approvingly.

Most of the women stopped chattering and lowered their paddles, eyeing Ally like she was some sort of criminal. The bidding slowed considerably, only Ally and two other women still in the running. She was raising her paddle, the bid increasing minimally each time.

Travis was giving her pained look, so she shouted again, "Three hundred thousand." She tried hard not to hyperventilate.

The other two women lowered their paddles and gave her cutting looks. But Ally ignored them because Travis looked happy as the auctioneer did a last call.

"One million dollars." The feminine call came from behind Ally, and she whipped around to see a beautiful brunette giving her a smug look.

Confused, Ally looked back up at Travis, but he wasn't looking at her. He was smiling at the beautiful brunette behind her. And the woman was looking right back at Travis now with a broad smile.

Ally waited, the whole room silent as the beautiful woman and Travis smiled at each other. When Travis's eyes finally moved back to her, he shook his head, and Ally looked at him in shock. Obviously, he wanted this woman to win the auction.

Pain radiated through Ally's chest and she tried to take a deep breath, but she found all she could do was breathe hard and fast, her chest aching as she watched the auctioneer award Travis to the gorgeous brunette.

The woman pushed past Ally, working her way to the front of the stage, not appearing to care who she pissed off in the process. As Travis stepped down, the woman flung herself into his arms, and Ally stepped back when she saw that Travis didn't rebuff her. He leaned down to whisper something in her ear, and the woman laughed and kissed him on the cheek, still clinging to his arm.

He wants her. He's not pushing her away. He wanted her to win the auction. He'll spend the whole night with her.

Ally turned and dropped her paddle to the floor, unable to watch Travis and the other woman any longer. At that moment, all she wanted to do was escape.

She pushed past the back of the crowd, looking desperately for a place to escape. Her face burned with humiliation and her heart clenched with hurt.

Could I have been so wrong about Travis?

Bolting through the outside door of the resort, she wandered blindly, ending up at the enormous hot springs pool that was now closed. There wasn't another soul around, so she sat in one of the wooden chairs beside the pool, the smell of minerals bringing back images of her and Travis making love in the pool at the guesthouse. She'd thought they'd been so connected, like there was no other person in the world for either one of them.

She tried to make sense of what had just happened, how Travis had turned away from her so easily, but she couldn't. And who the hell was the woman? Was she someone from his past? Ally had never seen her before, and what would a woman from his past be doing in Colorado?

He comes here a lot. Maybe he met her on a previous trip.

Whatever the case may be, Ally knew things would never be the same for her and Travis, and she was devastated. He'd picked another woman over her, and that pain was so intense that she wanted to curl up in a fetal position from the sheer agony. Tears poured down her face, and she let out a strangled sob just as she heard the distinctive ring of her phone.

She almost ignored it, but she pulled it out of her purse, noticing in the dim light that it was a call from home, the police department. She clicked the Talk button with trepidation.

The conversation that followed turned Ally's whole word upside down, leaving her feeling raw and completely destroyed by the time she clicked the phone back off. Her entire body shuddered and she froze in the chair, so shocked that she couldn't move.

"Ally?" Tate Colter took a seat beside her, but Ally barely noticed him. "You okay?"

She opened her mouth to speak, but the only thing that came out was, "No. I don't think so."

Tate leaned forward and put his elbows on his knees, waiting patiently. "Do you want to tell me about it?"

She wanted to tell someone, but she could barely comprehend the whole thing herself. "My house is gone. Apparently there was a sinkhole that opened underneath the house. They said it wasn't very big, but it was enough to crack the foundation and cause a leak in some of the pipes and lines. The gas leaked and the house exploded. It's entirely...gone." Saying the words made it seem more real. "I think Travis—"

"Saved your life?" Tate finished for her casually. "I'm sure he knew. He's been insistent on bringing you here for a while now."

"You know?" Ally looked at Tate in surprise.

"I've known for a while now. He saved my life, too. Back when I was on active duty, Travis warned me not to volunteer for any missions that I wasn't actually assigned to be on. I thought he was crazy. He knew very little about what I was doing. Nobody did, and they still don't. It's not something I can really talk about. All I can really say is that his warning made me hesitate when another pilot got sick and someone needed to take his place. I hesitated because of what Travis told me, because I wasn't assigned to it. And because I took a fraction of a second to think about what Travis said, somebody else spoke up before me and took the sick guy's place." He hesitated for a moment before adding solemnly, "Everyone on that mission died, Ally. When he told me about his dream about Asha, I took him seriously, and was more than happy to stay close to her. I didn't doubt that she was in some kind of danger if Travis had dreamed about it." Tate took her trembling hand in his. "I'm sorry about your house, Ally. But I'm glad you're here." He stroked her fingers lightly. "Travis is looking for you. He's worried."

"He has another date," Ally said painfully, her whole world still rocking from shock.

"The woman who bought him was my sister, Chloe, who happens to be engaged. She wanted to donate anyway, so she said she'd try to get here in time to bid on Travis since she wouldn't have to spend the evening with him. She won't stay long since she hates these kinds of functions. She hasn't seen him in a while and he cares about her like a sister. She didn't know about you, Ally. I didn't mention you. I just told her that Travis was helping out a friend and wasn't thrilled about taking his place. She said if she got here in time she'd do it. I never got a chance to tell her that you'd probably be bidding on him, too. It's not his fault. And he'd never do that to you. I've known Travis since college, and he's never cared about a woman the way he cares about you. He's frantic right now because he can't find you."

Tears of relief rolled down Ally's cheeks, and she started openly sobbing. Tate reached for her and put his arms around her shoulders, comforting her as she wept.

"You'll get another house, Ally. Everything will be okay," he crooned softly to her. "I know this is all a lot to take in, and you've lost everything, but it can all be replaced. You're still alive, and that's all that matters."

"It's just a house, and I didn't lose everything I care about. I still have Travis." She sniffled against his shoulder. The house was a shock, as was the fact that she could have very well been dead right now. What were the chances of a sinkhole opening underneath her house? She would have been home, probably already in bed. It was a pretty eerie feeling. But knowing Travis hadn't betrayed her was all she cared about right now. Her tears were now tears of relief rather than sorrow.

"I don't think you could lose Travis even if you tried," Tate said with a chuckle. "He's tearing the ballroom apart, looking for you."

Ally pulled back and gave Tate a weak smile. "Go tell him you found me. I'll be in. I just need a few minutes. I'm kind of a mess."

Tate got up and grinned at her wickedly. "I'll tell him we just finished a rendezvous in the dark."

"I wouldn't," Ally warned Tate.

"I would. I've never seen Travis like this before. It's highly entertaining," Tate retorted mischievously, whistling softly as he walked away.

Ally shook her head, wondering if Tate was suicidal as she watched him saunter away. Just then, her cell phone rang again.

Chapter 17

T ravis was frantic, ready to turn the ballroom upside down, when Tate wandered over to him, motioning with his thumb toward the door that led outside as he approached. "She's outside by the hot springs. She said she needed a few minutes."

What the hell? Why had she gone outside? Travis frowned at Tate, but didn't say a word as he started striding toward the door, but he didn't make it very far before Tate snagged his biceps with an iron grip.

"You need to calm down, Trav. Something bad happened to her tonight. Her house was destroyed, burned to the ground. She's upset," Tate said solemnly.

Tate's words hit Travis like a ton of bricks. "It really happened. Fuck!" His big body shuddered as he realized that his dream really had been precognitive, and Ally would most likely be dead had he not brought her to Colorado. Not that he would have taken any chances anyway, but it was an eerie and terrifying feeling, one that sent a cold chill down his spine. He yanked his arm out of Tate's grip and sprinted for the door, his heart thundering in his chest.

She's okay. She's okay.

Rationally, he knew that she was alive. Tate had just seen her. Still, he needed to see her beautiful face with his own eyes. And she needed him. He could sense it.

He spotted her standing beside the hot springs, just holding her phone in her hand and staring at the water. Jesus! She looked so lost and alone, and so damn vulnerable, her arms wrapped around her upper body, her face streaked with dark lines. She'd obviously been crying and her makeup and mascara outlined the marks of her tears. But she'd never looked more beautiful because she was standing right there, still alive and breathing.

She's mine. She was always supposed to be mine.

Travis had never been more certain of anything in his entire life. He wasn't the type of man who believed in fate, always believing that everyone made their own destiny. Now, he didn't believe that. Not when it came to Ally. There had really only ever been her, and he'd nearly lost her.

"Ally," he said hoarsely as he walked to her slowly, opening his arms as she turned at the sound of his voice. She flung her whole body toward him, and he closed his eyes as he folded her tightly into his embrace. "Everything will be okay, sweetheart. I'll make everything right again." He stroked his hand over her hair, holding her head tightly against his shoulder. "All that matters is that you're okay. Anything else, including the house, can be replaced."

"Tate told you?" Ally asked softly.

"Yeah."

"You knew it was going to happen, didn't you? That's why you wanted me to come with you? It didn't have anything to do with avoiding the auction. You were trying to save me."

"I had the same dream every time, but it was so fucking vague. I recognized the resort and the ballroom when I got a call that you had—" Travis had to force the word out his mouth in a guttural tone as he finished, "died. I didn't know how or why. I didn't know when. The only thing that made sense was that if something was going to happen, it was going to occur while I was in Colorado."

"Why didn't you tell me?" she asked in a confused voice.

"Christ, Ally. I wasn't even sure anything was going to happen. And I couldn't stand to even think about it, much less talk about it. I didn't want to scare you for no reason. But I was going to make damn sure you were in Colorado with me, even if I had to kidnap you."

"You wouldn't," she exclaimed, pulling back to look at his face. "And I might have been married."

Travis gripped the hands on her back into tight fists. It was past time that he stopped bullshitting himself and everyone else. "You wouldn't have married him. I would have done whatever I needed to do to make sure you didn't get married." He'd finally said it, admitted it to himself. It didn't matter how much he wanted to think he'd let her be happy with another man. It simply wouldn't have happened. He wanted her too much, needed her too much. He would have thrown her over his shoulder at the wedding if necessary and taken her away. "I couldn't have waited much longer. I would have done everything in my power to make you mine." His conviction that she belonged with him had been too strong, too powerful to ignore. The closer her wedding had gotten, the more desperate he had felt. There was no damn way he'd have let her say "I do" to another man without first fighting with everything he had to make her belong to him. Maybe he'd have fought with himself right up until the last moment, but he had no doubt how things would have ended, and she wouldn't have ended up married to someone else. He would have fought dirty if he'd had to, and he was perfectly capable of doing just that. "Hell, and I thought Sutherland was crazy for the plan he's making up with Tate's help. I would have done something just as crazy or worse."

"You never said what they were planning. You just said Jason was going after the woman he loved," Ally murmured.

"Believe me, you don't want to know," Travis told her emphatically, immediately changing the subject. "Tell me what happened with the house."

Ally explained what had happened, that she'd spoken to the police twice, and the house was a total loss. "I don't think it will really sink in until I see it," she finished sadly. "And I'll need to find a place to live. I can't believe I'm currently homeless."

"You're going to be living with me," Travis growled, his protective instincts sharp and nearly painful.

"I appreciate you giving me a place to stay for a while, but I'll find something as quickly as I can," she assured him gratefully.

Fuck! The woman was going to drive him insane. "Permanently, Ally. No finding another place."

Travis watched as she worried her lower lip, the dark smudges from her mascara still under her eyes. She was silent for a moment, the longest damn minute that Travis had ever endured before she replied, "I'm not sure I can do that, Travis."

He exploded. "The hell you can't. Why not?"

"Because I'm in love with you," she replied breathlessly. "I didn't mean for it to happen, but I love you. When I realized just a short time ago that if not for your warning, I would have been dead, all I could think about was that I would have regretted not telling you that. So I have to say it. But I also know how I felt when that beautiful brunette won the auction, and I knew you wanted her to when you hugged her. Just seeing you with another woman like that destroyed me. I know who she is now because Tate explained, but I realized that with you it has to be all or nothing for me. I love you so much it hurts," she ended on a sob.

Travis grasped both sides of her head and covered her mouth with his, kissing her roughly, his tongue taking possession of hers, melding them together as his head spun from her confession. *She fucking loved him.* He couldn't wrap his mind around that, and he didn't want to. Right now he wanted to brand her as his, let her know that they were never going to end. Finally, he pulled his mouth from hers and rasped, "Do you think I don't feel the same fucking way you do, Ally? I can't believe you thought for even a second that I could or would betray you. You can feel what I feel. I know you do. Do you really think I'd ever let you go? You're marrying me, and then I'll show you every damn day how lucky I feel to have you as mine." He moved his hands to her ass in a proprietary manner, desperately needing to bury his aching cock inside her. "I'm not sure love even explains how I feel. Dammit…I love you, but it's more than that.

I knew four years ago, from the minute you walked into my office and looked at me with those damn gorgeous green eyes of yours, that I was completely screwed, and not in a good way. So put me out of my misery after years of hell. Tell me you're going to marry me," he rasped, one of his hands slipping into her sexy panties, his fingers immediately drenched.

Ally moaned softly and answered, "But we haven't even talked about marriage yet," she protested weakly.

"Say it," Travis demanded in a husky voice, needing to hear her finally say she'd be with him forever. If she didn't, he was going to lose it. He teased her clit, putting more pressure on the bundle of nerves. "Say it now."

"Travis." His named left her lips with a sigh. "I love you."

Okay…he loved that, and he wanted to keep hearing her say it, but he wanted more. "Say you'll marry me." His patience at an end, he grasped the panties and tore them from her body, shoving them hastily into his pocket, as he pushed her back against the wall of the building, a dark, secluded corner where they wouldn't be seen.

"Travis, we can't do this here," Ally protested weakly. "And yes, I'll marry you. I love you."

Ah…both of the things he wanted to hear at once. Adrenaline pumped through him, his body and mind on such an ecstatic high that he never wanted to descend. There was no way he wasn't going to bury his cock inside her right now. He teased her clit a little harder, stroking the slick flesh between her thighs to make her even hotter as he liberated his cock from his pants. "Right now, Ally. I want to bury my cock inside you so deep that you can't think about anything but me fucking you and making you come."

"God, yes," she moaned. "Fuck me, Travis."

Shit. He loved hearing those words coming from her lips when his name was attached to them. He grasped her ass and pinned her to the wall as he lifted her. "Wrap your legs around my waist."

She obeyed immediately, fisting her hands into his hair as she said in a lusty, sultry voice, "You're mine, Travis."

Travis impaled her with one thrust of his cock, biting back a groan, loving the way she claimed him. Her possessiveness heated his blood, made his own proprietary emotions even more frenzied. There was nothing he wanted more than for her to feel secure enough, fierce enough to lay claim to him. "Tell me you love me," he demanded, wanting to hear those words all the time now that she'd said them.

"I love you. Now fuck me," she ordered, wrapping her arms securely around his shoulders.

Travis lost it, unable to keep himself from thrusting deep and hard inside her over and over again, the dark beast inside him taking control.

Need her to be mine. Need her to be mine.

"Tell me you'll stay with me forever," he commanded as he drove his cock into her deeper, harder, faster.

"Yes. Forever," she answered ferociously as her body started to quiver, her channel clamping down on his cock.

Travis could feel her climax tearing through her body, her channel pulsating over his pummeling cock. He grasped her ass harder, bringing her hips up to meet every stroke of his cock.

And then, she bit him, her teeth sinking into the flesh of his shoulder, which he knew was to keep herself from screaming. But the feel of her erotic marking made him detonate, and he moved his head and captured her mouth with his, both of them groaning into the kiss as they shuddered together, their muffled sounds of satisfaction mingling as their bodies were sated.

Releasing Ally's mouth so she could breathe, Travis buried his face in her hair as she rested her head on his shoulder, both of them gasping for breath. He lowered her feet to the ground, pulling her short skirt back around her thighs and fixing his trousers quickly before reaching for her again, keeping her locked against him.

"My wish came true," he told her in a hoarse voice.

"What wish?" Ally asked curiously, still slightly breathless.

"The one I made in the hot springs the other night."

"You wished you could screw me blind against a wall?" she asked teasingly. "And my wish came true, too."

Well…maybe if he had thought of that, he might have wished for it. It had been pretty damn amazing. But what he had wished for was much more important. "No. I wanted you to love me and stay with me forever."

She looked up at him, her luminous eyes filled with tears. "That was my wish. I wanted you to love me so badly."

Ally's words echoed in Travis's heart, and as he looked down at her, he vowed to give her all the love she'd never had in her life until now. She wanted so little when he wanted to give her so damn much. "I do. I wanted you to love me too, baby." He swiped at the tears rolling down her cheeks, making an even bigger mess of her makeup. He reached into his pocket, grinning as he came to her ripped panties first, but digging deeper for the small box he'd been hoping to give her tonight. He popped open the lid, the glimmering diamond catching every ray of the dim light. "I'm not even going to ask you to marry me again because you already said yes and you can't take it back," he grumbled, not willing to even take that chance. He pulled the ring from the box, put the container back in his pocket and took her hand, slipping the diamond onto her finger.

Mine.

Holy hell, she looked good wearing his ring, a physical declaration that she was finally his.

"Travis, I don't know what to say," she murmured, her eyes traveling from the ring to Travis's face. "Damn. All I've done is cry all night. I hardly ever cry." But her eyes were bright with tears.

"Nothing," Travis answered in a rush. "Don't say anything. You already said yes." No backing out now. She'd already agreed to marry him. There was nothing more to say. "Just kiss me," he suggested hopefully, hoping she wasn't going to cry again. "I don't want to see you sad anymore," he admitted in a ragged voice.

Ally stroked his cheek, and then put her hand behind his neck to give him the sweetest kiss he'd ever had. He savored it, savored an embrace that was full of tenderness and love, a connection that was so much more than passion. She pulled away slowly and whispered huskily, "I'm not sad. I'm overwhelmed."

"I know. Your house—"

"Not the house," she interrupted, giving him a small smile. "I'm overwhelmed by you, by us. I've never been this happy and it's almost scary."

"Then get used to being terrified, because I plan to keep you happy ever damn day," he answered with a devilish grin, knowing exactly how she felt. For a man who had lived in isolation and darkness for so long, being this damn happy was fucking terrifying, but he'd risk it. "You'll get used to it eventually."

Ally gave him a watery smile, swiping her hands across her cheeks. "I need to clean up. I know I'm a mess. And I'm curious to see who ended up with Tate for the evening."

Travis wasn't curious, but he smirked as he hoped the other man had ended up with the most annoying woman at the charity event. It would serve the bastard right for the way Tate had tortured him about Ally.

He put his arm around her and walked her to the ladies' room, waiting outside after he ducked into the men's room to clean himself up, propping a shoulder against the wall as he watched the crowd. The ball was in full swing, the auction apparently over. His eyes searched the dance floor, looking for Tate, but he didn't see him anywhere.

"I think I look as good as I'm going to get without more makeup," Ally said in a low, anxious voice behind him.

Travis turned and looked at her. "You're stunning." And she was the most beautiful woman he'd ever seen.

Ally rolled her eyes at him. "I look like a woman who has been crying all night. My eyes are puffy, my makeup is gone, and my nose is red. I'm not an attractive sight."

Travis thought she was wrong. He looked down at the ring on her finger and back up at her face, thinking she looked incredible. "You look like you're mine," he told her simply, thinking that *that* made her more than attractive. She looked like a goddamn miracle to him. "Dance with me," he demanded, reaching his hand out for hers.

She slipped her hand into his with a smile, moving closer to him to whisper, "Don't forget that my butt is bare. Some barbarian ripped off my panties and I doubt they're wearable."

They weren't. Travis had pretty much shredded them. He checked her skirt, making certain she was covered. "For Christ's sake, don't bend over," he rasped harshly, pulling her into a more secluded area of the dance floor, torn between the desire to hold her in his arms and his territorial need to make sure he didn't expose her. As he pulled her into his arms, he solved the problem by putting one of his hands on her ass instead of her back, making damn sure her skirt didn't ride up.

"People are staring," Ally told him in an amused voice as she followed his lead perfectly.

"I don't give a shit," he responded, surprising himself that he really didn't care. It was a formal occasion, and maybe it wasn't appropriate to hold her this way, but it felt good. "If they don't like it, they don't have to look."

"Travis Harrison, are you actually willing to do something a little bit scandalous?" Ally teased.

He looked into her deep green eyes, his expression intense. "There's nothing I wouldn't do when it comes to you," he told her in a hoarse rasp, knowing he meant every single word. "Tell me you love me again," he said insistently, knowing he sounded pathetic, but he didn't care about that either.

"I love you," she responded immediately.

Travis felt his cock growing hard just from the tender, sultry tone of her words. Unable to stop himself, he stopped dancing and he kissed her, not holding back anything as he tried to tell her without words how much he treasured that love. Ally loved him exactly as he was, asshole and all. She didn't care about his wealth, his freaky precognitive dreams, or his less than tactful behavior sometimes. She just cared about…him.

Cameras flashed, and Travis knew he'd see a picture of himself in the society pages tomorrow, ravishing his new fiancée on the dance floor of a charity ball. And he'd actually relish it. He'd waited for Ally for years, and he wanted every man in the world to know she now belonged to him. In fact, he'd happily look for the photo tomorrow because he was pretty damn sure he'd frame it.

Chapter 18

One week later, Ally watched Travis's face as he painfully explained to his family the truth about his precognitive dreams, knowing how difficult it was for him. Her heart ached as she sat on the arm of his chair in his living room, his family all listening intently, as though they could sense how difficult this was for him, too.

Max and Mia were seated on the loveseat, Kade and Asha on the couch, all of them completely silent for a few moments after Travis stopped speaking.

"I knew," Kade finally said, his voice low and uncharacteristically sad. "I didn't know you were having dreams, and I couldn't really figure everything out, but I knew everything that happened was more than coincidence. You were there almost every damn time we needed you. Why the hell didn't you tell me the whole truth? That's a hell of a burden to have to bear alone, Trav."

"I couldn't tell you," Travis answered in a tortured voice, scrubbing his face with his hands. "You and Mia were all I had, and our father was insane. I didn't want anyone to think I was as crazy as he was. I just wanted us all to be normal again." He paused for a minute before adding, "I didn't dream about your accident, Kade. I'm sorry."

Kade rose, his face set in a grim expression. He walked to Travis's chair and said adamantly, "Get up."

Ally cringed, hoping she wasn't going to regret talking Travis into telling his family everything. This was her doing, her idea completely. She loved Travis so much, and she wanted him to bridge the distance with his siblings. Ally knew they loved him just as much as he loved them, although he'd never expressed himself well because of his isolation, and right now Travis needed assurances. She just wanted him to be happy, to realize how special he was, and she was counting on his siblings to help.

She watched as Travis slowly got to his feet, staring at his twin's somber face, his expression uncertain. It took Kade less than a second to wrap his older brother into one of the fiercest bear hugs Ally had ever seen.

"I love you, you asshole," Kade said ferociously, hugging Travis tightly in his beefy arms. "And you could never be like our father. You're the glue that held this family together every single time we needed it. I don't give a shit if you couldn't tell me about the accident. I wouldn't be with the woman I love more than life if it hadn't happened. Sometimes our pain in life is worth it."

Ally watched, tears rolling down her cheeks as Travis slowly responded, and she saw his big body shudder as he hugged Kade in return, the two of them locked together in a brotherly embrace. She didn't need to be told that it was the first time Kade had ever felt free to really express how much he cared about Travis because Travis had always kept everyone at a distance in the past.

"I love you, too, little brother," Travis answered quietly, slapping Kade on the back as they separated.

Ally's heart clenched as she watched Kade's face turn into a happy grin as Mia came right up behind him and threw herself into Travis's arms, her face wet with tears. "I'm so sorry, Travis. So sorry for everything. If I hadn't gotten myself into trouble, you and Kade wouldn't have been so distant with each other while I was hiding out in Montana. Max and Kade had each other. You didn't have anybody," she choked out on a sob, clinging to her older brother like a lifeline.

"I did, Mia," Travis crooned, holding his sister and rocking her. "I had you. At least I knew you were alive. I didn't have to deal with the hell that I put Kade and Max through because they thought you were dead."

"I would have been if you hadn't hidden me and kept quiet," Mia answered, finally pulling back and kissing Travis on the cheek. "Max, Kade, and I would all be dead. You already know I love you, but I don't think you'll ever know how much. I've caused you the most problems, yet I still know you care." Mia swiped at her tears as she stepped back, looking her brother in the face.

"I love you, Mia. I always have. And I'm your big brother. It's my job to keep you out of trouble," Travis told her almost arrogantly, but he was smiling.

Asha was the next to get her hugs and kisses in with Travis, and Max came forward and shook Travis's hand and slapped him on the back in a brief hug. Stepping back from Travis, Max said remorsefully, "I owe you an apology, Travis. I hate myself for this, but I've resented you since I learned you hid Mia away from me."

Max returned to take his seat by Mia, and Travis sat back down. Ally reached out her hand and Travis clasped it, bringing her palm to his lips and kissing it tenderly before bringing their joined hands to rest on the arm of the chair.

"I know you did, Max. And I knew to this day you were still resentful. But I never blamed you," Travis answered honestly.

"I'm not anymore, Travis. I am so damn grateful, and I don't know how to say thanks for saving every one of us," Max answered thoughtfully.

"I can't believe you all just accept this, that you believe me," Travis said hoarsely.

Ally squeezed his hand, knowing that his family's unconditional acceptance meant everything to him.

"Why wouldn't we?" Asha asked curiously. "When Tate rescued me, he told me that you texted him. How did you know I needed him?"

"I had a vague dream the night before," Travis admitted. "And I wasn't feeling good about the whole situation." He shrugged. "It happens that way sometimes."

"You have an incredible gift, Travis. I think there are many spiritual things that we don't understand, but it doesn't mean that they don't exist," Asha murmured. "I'm more grateful than you'll ever know that you texted Tate that day. I wouldn't have made it even a few minutes longer without his help."

Ally wanted to hug her friend for reassuring Travis, for trying to make him more comfortable with himself. "He saved Tate, too."

Mia leaned forward, a look of awe on her face. "Tell us."

"He told you?" Travis asked, looking up at her with a frown.

"He did. When my house was destroyed, he told me his story because I told him I thought you knew it was going to happen."

Ally quickly explained what had happened with Tate to the rest of the family. Travis had already told them about his recurring dreams about Ally, and why he'd taken her to Colorado.

"Holy shit, Trav. That's amazing," Kade exclaimed, gaping at Travis.

"It's peculiar. And so am I," Travis rumbled awkwardly, but not very emphatically.

Ally sighed, knowing it would take time for Travis to completely accept who he was, but having his family know about it and validate him was an important step.

"You're gifted," Asha argued.

"Special," Mia said with a nod.

"I never wanted to be gifted or special," Travis rasped. "After our crazy childhood and our insane father, I just wanted to be normal."

"You've never been normal," Kade said with a grin. "You've always been an asshole. And what happened to the brother who told me he hadn't met a woman who was worth losing his common sense over? Did you see the picture of you in the paper grabbing Ally's butt and kissing her like you'd lost it in the middle of a formal ball?"

"Yep. I framed it and it's on my desk at work," he admitted non-apologetically. "I've joined the psycho men club. In fact, I might have to become the damn president of the organization."

"Still want to get rid of that desk?" Kade asked with a smirk.

"Hell, no. Not anymore. It's become my favorite damn piece of furniture in the whole building," he answered emphatically.

Ally flushed, knowing exactly why Travis used to hate that desk. But they'd had a few more adventures in the office on that particular wood surface, and now he swore he'd keep it forever, even if it did distract him sometimes. But she knew he'd be cursing it again if she wasn't around.

The men bantered a little longer, the women throwing in their own comments.

Ally looked down at Travis, finally breathing a sigh of relief. Today had been a big hurdle for him, and she knew he hadn't really wanted to deal with it. But she had enough faith in his family to know that they'd always accepted Travis unconditionally, and she wanted him to know that, to believe that. So she had pushed him, encouraged him, hoping nothing would go wrong. Someday he'd be more comfortable with his special and unique traits, but he'd lived with his gift alone for so long that it wouldn't happen overnight.

She'd been staying with him since they'd returned from Colorado, and although his house was enormous and had incredible security, it wasn't ostentatious. Of course, she should have known it wouldn't be, because that wasn't Travis's style.

He'd gone to her destroyed house with her, but almost nothing was recoverable. Strangely, she wasn't really sad. There were a few personal items that she would have liked to have, but it was almost like she hadn't even really started living until she'd fallen in love with Travis. And it felt like everything that had happened before in her life was all leading to this…to him. Travis made her feel loved, complete, and perfect. She doubted they'd ever stop fighting some-times, but it was almost like…foreplay. Besides, Travis wasn't the type of man who needed a wife who didn't challenge him. And she adored his loving alpha male, protective personality. It made her feel safe, and there was never a day that she didn't feel loved, even if he was pissed off at her for something.

"So when is the wedding?" Asha asked inquisitively, looking excitedly at Ally.

"Soon," Travis said irritably.

"Next year," Ally answered at the same time.

They looked at each other and frowned.

Travis wrapped a steely arm around her waist and pulled her into his lap. "I'm not waiting until next year," he informed her stubbornly, his voice holding a warning note.

"We haven't set a date yet," she told Asha with a wink.

"But it sure as hell won't be next year," Travis replied obstinately.

Kade looked at Max. "Should we start placing bets on who will win this argument?"

"Nope," Max replied with a grin. "It wouldn't work. We'd both be betting on Travis."

Asha, Kade, Max, and Mia all laughed as they got up to leave.

"I think we'll let you two work this one out," Kade said, slapping Travis on the back as he walked past him.

Ally scrambled to get off Travis's lap to see everyone out, but he held her tightly for a minute longer, whispering huskily into her ear, "We aren't waiting that long, even if I have to get out my naughty tie."

Ally shivered at the thought, knowing that when Travis wanted something, he always got it. When Travis really wanted to be wicked, he knew exactly how to get to her. "We'll discuss it," she told him firmly as she got up.

"Not for long," Travis said ominously, a happy grin on his face now.

Ally smiled back, more than ready to bicker with him because it always ended in the most delicious make-up sex.

Finally, Travis closed the door behind his family and faced her, a look of relief on his face.

"Was it so hard?" Ally asked him tenderly, knowing it had been, and wondering if he wanted to talk about it.

"You were right. I needed to do it," he answered in a voice husky with emotion. He pulled her against him, wrapping his arms tightly around her and burying his face in her hair. "Thank you for giving me back my family, Ally." His voice was coarse and raw with emotion.

Ally tried to swallow the lump that was forming in her throat as Travis held her tightly, his body quaking. She stroked his hair, wrapping her other arm around his neck, knowing how much all this meant to him. He'd been alone for so very long, having a family but yet never quite being connected to them since the death of his parents. Ally was so grateful that everyone in Travis's family had tried to convince him that his parents' deaths weren't his fault. "I love you," she told him gently, continuing to stroke his hair to comfort him.

"I love you so much I think it might kill me," Travis said in a muffled voice, still not loosening his grip on her. "You need to marry me soon," he added in a more demanding but poignant voice.

"We'll talk about it," Ally said, knowing she'd relent. She felt the same way as Travis did, and she didn't want to wait.

Travis pulled back and met her gaze, his expression intense. "Like hell we will," Travis grunted.

And then he kissed her, and Ally knew exactly who was going to win this argument as she was swept away by the same volatile passion he was feeling, the two of them completely lost in each other.

Epilogue

Two Months Later

Ally knew Travis was on his way, and she whispered her usual countdown.

"Five...

"Four...

"Three...

"Two...

"One..."

She sighed as she watched her handsome husband walk through the door of his office, dressed in one of her favorite dark suits, and shooting her the wickedly gorgeous grin that always made her heart start doing cartwheels inside her chest.

"Good morning, beautiful," he said gruffly, his eyes roaming over her possessively.

"Good morning, Mr. Harrison," she responded mischievously. "Let me get you some coffee." Ally was always willing to go get his coffee when he greeted her like *that*, which he hadn't failed to do on any day since they'd returned from Colorado.

Most days, they rode to work together, but Travis had had an early morning meeting, so Ally had driven herself in her new vehicle. Travis had gotten her a Ferrari F12 as a wedding gift, a surprise that she hadn't quite recovered from yet, although they'd been married a month ago in a small ceremony at his home. Even though the wedding had been small, it had been the most beautiful event of her life, the day she was joined with the man she knew she'd love forever and beyond. Asha, Mia, Maddie, and Kara had all pitched in to get it planned quickly, and they'd had all their family and closest friends at the ceremony and reception, which was everything Ally had ever wanted or dreamed of for a wedding. Of course, Travis had needed to have the best of everything for the wedding, and had shocked her later with a new F12.

Ally was pretty sure he was still anxious about her driving a fast car, and he'd texted her twice to make sure she'd made it safely to work, reminding her to watch her speed. If she was honest, she hadn't been able to resist using a little of the enormous power of the vehicle, but only reasonably so, because she was still a little nervous about driving a car that damn expensive.

Travis had taken her out to his racetrack, but Ally hadn't yet seen him use the superb racing skills that she knew he was capable of exhibiting when she was in the car. She teased him about driving like a little old man in some of his fastest cars, but he just grumbled that he wasn't risking her life by doing suicidal speeds when she was with him. But she loved the exhilarating feeling of speed when Travis was doing his track runs, even if she knew he drove a hell of a lot faster on them when she wasn't around.

Ally grabbed them both a cup of coffee and brought them into his office so they could have their morning discussion about business. She looked at him, his expression now pensive. "Are you okay?" Ally asked, concerned. He'd looked so happy a few minutes ago.

"I have something for you," he said slowly, his voice low and serious as he added, "Please don't get mad."

Ally quirked a brow at him, wondering if he was referring to some of her lectures about buying her things she didn't need. After her house had been destroyed, Travis bought, and bought, and bought for her, even when he knew she'd eventually get an insurance settlement to replace the things she really needed. And he hadn't stopped yet, many of the things he was buying way more than she needed.

"I probably won't get mad," Ally told him patiently, although she always left herself some wiggle room in case he went over the top.

"You might," Travis warned her, holding out an envelope to her. "This is for you."

A little alarmed by the serious expression on his face, she hopped up and took the letter, looking immediately at the return address, recognizing the name immediately. "Why would I be getting something from them?" she asked quietly, perplexed as she opened the envelope, and then slipped her reading glasses from the top of her head and put them on.

As she started reading the enclosed letter, her knees gave way and she had to sit to complete the rest of the correspondence. "Oh my God. This isn't real. It's a hoax." It was a notification that the first book in her young adult fantasy series had won one of the most prestigious awards possible for an unpublished manuscript. "I didn't ever submit to them."

"I did." Travis's voice was low and anxious. "But it was all you, Ally. None of the judges know who the manuscript belongs to and I swear I didn't interfere. I just submitted it. What does the letter say?"

Ally's eyes flew to his face, astonished. "It says I won first place, book of the year for an unpublished manuscript." Her hands were trembling as she got up and handed him the letter, watching as he scanned the brief notification.

He grinned up at her. "I knew you'd win."

If Travis was telling her he hadn't made this happen, that she had won on her own merit, she knew it was true. If there was one thing Travis didn't ever do, it was blatantly lie. He might have avoided the truth in the past, but he'd never lie to her about something like this. "You submitted for me?" Ally said huskily, her voice clogged with tears. Just the fact that Travis thought about doing something like that was amazing. She knew he had faith in her, but this was incredible.

"Are you angry?" He sounded nervous. "I know I should have asked you first, but I didn't think you'd do it. And I knew you'd win."

"I probably wouldn't have," Ally admitted, knowing she'd grown emotionally a great deal since she'd broken off her relationship with Rick. Still, submitting her manuscript for such a prestigious award would have been daunting, and it honestly probably wouldn't have even occurred to her to do so.

"I wanted you to have official validation that your work is fantastic from people who wouldn't be biased. People other than me."

Ally got up and walked around the desk, and threw her arms around his neck. He seized her body immediately, pulling her into his lap.

"I'm not mad," she told him tearfully, still so amazed at the strength and thoughtfulness of the man she had married.

"I just want you to be happy, Ally. I know you said you still wanted to stay here and work with me, but I want you to do whatever you want to do, reach for whatever dreams you have. You can finish your MBA, or write more award-winning novels now that everyone in publishing will be wanting to put out your books. I don't care what it takes to make you happy. I'll do it," Travis said fiercely, his grip tightening around her waist. "As long as you're always mine."

"I'm already ecstatically happy, Travis, because you love me." She brushed an errant lock of hair from his forehead. "And I don't want to go back to college for my MBA anymore. I think I was studying business because it was safe, normal. I do want to write, and I want to be with you and make you happy. Those are my only two dreams now. And someday I'd like to have a child."

"Sweetheart, I'm already happy. And I'm more than willing to do overtime to work on that baby dream," he told her enthusiastically.

Ally smiled, knowing if he worked any harder at *that*, she'd be exhausted. Travis was already insatiable. And really, she loved her job at Harrison now that her husband wasn't the billionaire boss from Hell anymore. "I'd like to stay, unless you want another assistant.

I can write in the evenings and weekends when you're busy. And you did promise me you'd take me everywhere with you. I can write anywhere."

"Thank God," Travis replied fervently, placing his forehead on her shoulder, relieved. "I doubt I could find anyone else to put up with me, and I wasn't sure how I'd make it through an entire day without you here. I need you, Ally."

Ally's heart clenched, knowing he meant that he needed her in more ways than just an assistant. And she needed him, too. Maybe as the two of them got used to their intense relationship that left them both feeling vulnerable, they'd feel differently. But right now, Ally was exactly where she wanted to be.

"I'd never get another job with such great fringe benefits," Ally told him teasingly. "And it would be sad if you started hating your desk again." She reached out and stroked a hand over the polished wood.

Travis growled and stood, lifting her onto the desk in front of him. "I think I need a reminder of just how much I love it." His expression was wicked as he started unbuttoning her blouse.

"Mr. Harrison, you have a meeting shortly," Ally reminded him sternly.

"They can wait. I'm the damn boss," he rasped.

Ally reached out and started unbuttoning his shirt, needing to touch his heated skin. "I need to touch you," she murmured, her heart so full of love that she was afraid it was going to burst.

"Fuck. Then I'll probably make it to the meeting on time," he said harshly. "You know what happens when you do that."

"Then kiss me," she asked him sweetly.

Travis looked down at her, his eyes dark and swirling with emotion. "I love you, Ally."

Her heart skipped a beat as she saw the intensity in his eyes as she replied, "I love you." She wrapped her arms around his neck, abandoning his buttons to sink into Travis's passionate embrace.

He was still late for his meeting, but when he finally did arrive, he shocked his employees by entering the conference room with an enormous smile on his face. Halfway through the meeting, Travis's phone blasted a loud, upbeat musical tone. Every face around the conference table was stunned when, instead of being irritated about Ally changing the ringtone on his phone...Travis Harrison actually laughed.

~*The End*~

Please visit me at:
http://www.authorjsscott.com
http://www.facebook.com/authorjsscott

You can write to me at
jsscott_author@hotmail.com

You can also tweet
@AuthorJSScott

Please sign up for my Newsletter for updates,
new releases and exclusive excerpts.

Books by J. S. Scott:

The Billionaire's Obsession Series:

The Billionaire's Obsession

Heart Of The Billionaire

The Billionaire's Salvation

The Billionaire's Angel
(part of a Duet – A Maine Christmas…Or Two)

The Billionaire's Game

Billionaire Undone

13005306R00118

Printed in Great Britain
by Amazon.co.uk, Ltd.,
Marston Gate.